A big shout-out THANK YOU
to some Super Fans:

Kim Baccellia
Michelle Gottier
Amelia Percival
Jennifer Rummel
Amanda M. Smith
Cynthia Leitich Smith
Rose Thomason

DEAD GIRL
DANCING

Linda Joy Singleton

Woodbury, Minnesota

Teen
F
Single

First Edition
Second Printing, 2010

Book design by Steffani Sawyer
Cover design by Gavin Dayton Duffy
Cover image © 2008 Agb/Shutterstock Images

Flux, an imprint of Llewellyn Publications

Library of Congress Cataloging-in-Publication Data
Singleton, Linda Joy.
  Dead girl dancing / Linda Joy Singleton.—1st ed.
      p. cm.—(Dead girl ; 2)
  Summary: High-schooler Amber's second assignment as a "Temp Lifer"
takes her into the body of her boyfriend's twenty-one-year-old sister
Shari, who has shut herself off from family and friends and gotten
involved with a "Dark Lifer."
  ISBN 978-0-7387-1406-6
  [1. Self-esteem—Fiction. 2. Emotional problems—Fiction.
3. Identity—Fiction. 4. Best friends—Fiction. 5. Friendship—Fiction.
6. Future life—Fiction.] I. Title.
  PZ7.S6177Ddm 2008
  [Fic]—dc22
                                                    2008044037

Flux
Llewellyn Publications
A Division of Llewellyn Worldwide Ltd.
2143 Wooddale Drive, Dept. 978-0-7387-1406-6
Woodbury, MN 55125-2989, U.S.A.
www.fluxnow.com

Printed in the United States of America

1

I could not believe I was in the wrong body—again!

Memo to self: Never make a promise to a dead grandmother.

Last I knew, I was talking to Grammy Greta via an out-of-body experience. She said I had a talent for helping people and I'd make a good Temp Lifer. On the other side, my grandmother has this important job as an Earthbounder Counselor—she gives humans in crisis a time-out from their lives by sending in temporary replacements. I was so flattered by her praise that I'd promised to help her any time. But I hadn't expected her to switch me into someone else's body right away—especially the body of my boyfriend's sister, Sharayah.

Standing in front of a full length mirror, I stared at shoulder length dark hair, curved cheek bones, an eyebrow ring and shocked eyes. Transforming from a high schooler to a college girl didn't sound bad in theory; being mature and of legal age for a few days could be a cool experience. But being my boyfriend's sister was *sooo* going to ruin my love life. Eli and I hadn't seriously kissed yet—and now even thinking about kissing him was illegal and immoral.

I mean, how could I make out with my boyfriend when I was his sister?

And where *was* Eli's sister? I wondered, frowning into the mirror at the pierced brow and blue eyes—not brown—staring back at me. Since I was here, did that mean Sharayah was in my body? Was she still in the coma, or waking up to the shock of her life? According to Grammy, Temp Lifers only replaced people who couldn't deal with their problems and were in crisis mode. What was Sharayah's crisis? And how was I supposed to help her when I didn't know how to help myself?

Seeing everything through a stranger's eyes tilted my equilibrium, distorting my senses. Nothing smelled the same and my skin fit uncomfortably, closer to the bones without the cushion of extra pounds. Swiveling my hips away from the mirror made me feel like a floppy doll yanked by puppeteer strings. I steadied myself on a dresser, my elbow brushing a digital clock that flashed 4:57 A.M. Almost morning? But it seemed like I'd only been sleeping a few minutes. If the clock was right, then not only had I lost my body—but also nearly twelve hours.

At least it was easy to guess where I was—in Sharayah's college dorm room. If the reflection in the mirror hadn't clued me in, there was the framed photo of the Rockingham family: Sharayah, her parents and brothers Chad and Eli. The room was only slightly bigger than a closet and clearly divided into two personalities. One side was all girly pink and organized, with matching satin pillows and a pink quilted comforter on a neatly made twin bed. A sharp contrast to the other side of the room—Sharayah's half, I assumed, since that was where I'd awakened. Her twin bed was tangled in blankets with piles of clothes and random stuff abandoned on the floor. There was an odd smell, too; a mix of sweat, perfume, and alcohol. When I inhaled, my stomach reeled and my throat ached with bitter dryness. I ached all over, too, like I'd jogged for a whole day (and I hate exercise). When I looked down at myself, I realized the baggy shirt I was wearing over a lacy red thong was a *guy's* shirt.

Who was the guy and how did I end up with his shirt?

This was *not* good.

What had Eli told me about his sister? I remembered his hurt expression when he'd talked about her sudden personality change: dropping friends, shutting out her family, and acting wild.

Exactly how wild? I worried.

I spotted a black leather handbag on the end table beside Sharayah's bed and started for it—then yelped when I bumped my foot on an empty wine bottle, which rolled under the bed and clinked like it had hit another bottle. Someone had been doing some serious partying … and I had a sick feeling it was me.

Did Sharayah's crisis have to do with too much partying? Or was she having romantic problems with her (shirtless) boyfriend? I couldn't even begin to guess until I found out more about her. So I opened the leather handbag and found a hair brush, an earring shaped like a skull, cherry lip gloss, an iPod, keys, a cell phone, and a wallet with Sharayah's driver's license showing she'd recently turned twenty-one. There were also two credit cards, a college ID, postage stamps, a restaurant receipt—and twelve hundred dollars in cash.

"Wow!" I exclaimed, flipping through the crisp green hundred-dollar bills.

Ordinarily, lots of money would inspire whoops for joy—instead, my worries multiplied. Why would a college girl carry around so much cash? I doubted it was for anything worthwhile like textbooks or tuition. And my thoughts darkened. I hated to suspect Sharayah of anything illegal—she was Eli's sister after all—and if she got in serious trouble, he'd be devastated. The crisp green bills seemed to burn my fingers. I dropped them back into the purse.

Picking up Sharayah's cell phone, I punched in Eli's cell number, envisioning him sleeping peacefully. My head throbbed so much there wasn't room for any guilt about waking him. This was an emergency and I needed him; that was all that mattered. Hurry, answer! I urged, listening to ringing as I walked over to Sharayah's family portrait, running my finger across the unruly curl of Eli's hair that waved across his forehead. Another lifetime ago (actually only a few days ago) I'd looked at a copy of this exact picture in Eli's room. He wasn't athletic or cover-model pretty like his brother Chad, but when I looked into his eyes, I saw loyalty, humor, intelligence...and I missed him.

"Huh?" Eli said groggily, after about eight rings.

"Eli!" My heart jumped at his voice. "I'm so glad you're there!"

"Who is … ohmygod! Sharayah! Is it really you?"

"Uh … sorry but no," I said in a lower-pitched, melodious voice I'd never heard before. "I'm not her."

"What are you talking about? Do you want to talk to Mom or Dad?"

"No! I called to talk to you."

"What is it? Are you in trouble?"

"Not exactly—but I'm afraid Sharayah is."

"Huh? What do you mean?"

"Eli, I'm not—" I sucked in a shaky breath. "I'm not your sister."

"No matter what you've done, Shari, you'll always be my sister. Nothing can be that bad and you know we're always here for you. Are you okay? Mom and Dad are worried sick, I mean, you didn't come home for Christmas! What were we supposed to think?"

"Eli … I know I sound like your sister … but it's Amber." I braced myself for his reply, knowing that being in the wrong body was unbelievable—but it wasn't like this was the first time. Only yesterday I'd been a wealthy, gorgeous, disturbed girl from school named Leah Montgomery. Eli knew to expect the unexpected with me. It was one of the many things I liked (maybe even loved) about him.

"Amber?" he repeated. "Amber Borden?"

"How many Ambers do you know?" I sighed. "It happened again."

"This isn't possible. You can't be Amber—she's still in the

hospital. I was with her yesterday until visiting hours ended, hoping she'd wake up, but she never did."

"That's because I'm not there anymore. I think Sharayah is taking my place. I was shocked when I woke up in your sister's dorm room—and her body."

"No way!"

"It's true. I can hardly believe it myself."

"But you can't be my sister!"

"Only on the outside," I told him. "Inside I'm still the same directionally challenged, chocolate-obsessed math geek. The last time I saw you—yesterday, I guess—we were in the hospital waiting for the magical switch from Leah's body to mine. After we kissed, I saw this dazzling light and talked to Grammy. I thought everything was going to be okay—until a few minutes ago."

"What went wrong?" he demanded. "Leah acted like she was herself again, but you just kept on sleeping and no one could wake you up—even the doctors couldn't figure it out."

I took a deep breath. "I'm a Temp Lifer."

"Huh? A what?"

"Temp Lifers are like body doubles—stepping in for the rough scenes when someone can't deal with their life role. Only instead of working for Hollywood, Temp Lifers report to the other side," I explained, although it was hard to describe something I didn't fully understand.

My grandmother had said Temp Lifers were usually souls who had passed over, except in rare cases when a living person (like me) helped out. As with anything good, there was a bad side, too: Dark Lifers. These renegade Temp Lifers hijacked human bodies to avoid returning to the light. I'd had a creepy encounter with one and never ever wanted to go through that again.

"Let me get this straight," Eli said, as if trying to be calm even though I could tell he was upset. "Instead of returning to your own body, you swapped with my sister?"

"Yes."

"So while I was waiting for you to wake up, holding your hand and saying... well, things I would never say to my sister... it was her and not you?"

"Um... yeah." I bit my lip. "But I doubt she heard you. She might not even be there. I don't really know how this all works. I swear I didn't know this was going to happen when I offered to help my grandmother. I didn't think she'd really switch me."

"You didn't think at all," he said bitterly. "Finally we hear from my sister and you're not even her."

"This sucks for me, too. I'm alone in a strange place instead of with my real family. I hoped to be back with them by now... and with you, too. I really miss you, Eli. I was looking forward to being in my own body and spending a lot of time with you."

"I wanted that too. Only now we can't... well... anything."

"Yeah. I freaked when I looked in the mirror and saw your sister. I mean, YOUR SISTER. How could Grammy do this to me?" Tears swelled in my eyes. "Everything is so messed up. I just want to be me again."

"Ask your grandmother to switch you back."

"Don't you think I would if I knew how?" I wiped my eyes and gold flashed from the elegant bracelet on my wrist.

It looked expensive, the sort of bling I dreamed of affording someday when I became a famous entertainment agent. But at that moment I'd give anything to wear my cheap "lucky" rainbow braided bracelet. Grammy said if I was ever in trouble to say a "magic" chant and twist the bracelet to contact her, but I didn't even know where the bracelet was. Without it, I was lost—literally.

"Isn't there anything you can do?" Eli asked me.

"Wait to hear from Grammy, I guess. She told me she's never far away. At least this is only a temporary job so once Sharayah rests a few days and is strong enough to deal with her problems, I should change back." I hope.

"Only a few days?" Eli sounded relieved. "That's not too bad . . . it could even turn out to be a good thing."

"Good?" I asked skeptically.

"Good for my family. My parents are really hurt because Sharayah won't visit or even talk to us."

"You said she didn't come for Christmas, so her problems started over three months ago?"

"At least," he said angrily. "A few weeks after Thanksgiving. We blame her boyfriend—some older guy named Gabe. She wouldn't tell us anything about him but everything changed when they started going out. She switched roommates—dumping Hannah who's been her closest friend since preschool. We heard from her other friends, too, wanting to know why she wasn't returning calls. The only time we heard from her was when she needed money."

"About money," I said, with an uneasy glance down at Sharayah's purse. "Does she . . . uh . . . have a job?"

"I doubt it. She's majoring in pre-med and her college

load is too heavy for anything except volunteering at clinics. But she's changed so much that I have no clue what she's been doing. Let me know what you find out. Now that I think about it, I'm glad you're there. If my sister is so stressed out she needs a temporary replacement, who better for the job?"

"Yay, me," I said with zero enthusiasm.

"You won't be alone. After I work out some details—like borrowing a car from my parents—I'll drive there."

"Really? You'll drive all the way to ... " I paused, realizing I didn't even know what city I was in.

"You're in San Jose," he said, chuckling.

That wasn't too far—only a few hours' drive. I suddenly felt much better. "I'll be here waiting. It's not like I can go anywhere else. I doubt I even have a car."

"Actually you do—if you can call that pint-sized Geo a car. Dad about had a heart attack when Shari bought that car instead of getting something from his dealership. That was only the beginning of her problems."

"She'll be okay," I assured him.

"But will you?" he asked, so sympathetically that I felt like crying and had to swallow hard to stay calm.

I didn't know how to answer; I was reluctant to admit I was scared and worried I'd screw up Sharayah's life as well as my own. I wanted Eli's respect, not his pity, and the self-help books I studied advised stuff like "nothing is sexier than confidence" and "never show fear." So I assured him everything was fine, that I would do a great job as a Temp Lifer and successfully solve Sharayah's problems.

For a moment I actually believed I could do this—like I was Super Amber and could achieve anything. But I guess my super powers didn't include talking with guys, because there was this awkward silence between us, as if we were both waiting for the other to say something romantic. But who knew if there even was an "us"? We hadn't gone out on a real date, since I'd spent most of our time together in someone else's body.

"Well … um … " I finally said oh-so-not-brilliantly.

"I better … you know … go," he said, just as brilliantly.

"You should … I guess."

"I guess … but Amber?"

"Yes? Yes?" My heart fluttered.

"I just want to say … "

"What?"

"That I … I … "

My cell phone beeped, flashing an incoming text message. I swore at the stupid timing of the stupid call, then realized Eli might think I was swearing at him and started to apologize as I hit the "stop" button to prevent another stupid beep from interrupting my conversation. Only the phone was a newer model than I'd ever used before and instead of shutting off the beep, I hung up on Eli.

Damn! Not the romantic way I wanted to end our conversation. I considered calling him back, but didn't want to go through that whole awkward good-bye thing again. Besides he'd be here in a few hours and then we'd talk—really talk.

The text message indicator kept flashing, so I hit a few buttons until one seemed to work. There was no name of the sender, only an unknown phone number and a short message:

I M WATCHING U.

I flung the phone across the room like it was on fire. Then I raced over to the window with acute paranoia. The blinds were drawn but not completely closed, so I peered through them, seeing only inky night and the dim glow of street lights. Except for the faint noise of distant traffic, the night world was still and silent. But anyone could lurk in the dark; uninvited, unseen ... unfriendly.

Was someone out there staring up at me?

Grabbing the blind's cord, I shut out the night, yanking so hard the cord dug into my palm. But I hardly noticed the pain as I sagged against a desk, my pulse racing. No one could see inside now so I should be safe ... only I didn't feel safe.

It was just a crank message, I assured myself. Still, I had

this prickly sensation in the back of my neck—why threaten me? But what was I thinking? This wasn't about me. This phone belonged to Sharayah. So the text was meant for her—probably a friend messing around or the "shirtless" boyfriend's perverted idea of flirting.

Yet the words "I M WATCHING U" were stalkerish, scaring me almost as much as when I'd been threatened by a Dark Lifer. I didn't really expect a Dark Lifer to appear in the dorm room, but fear created paranoia. What if it was a Dark Lifer? Their dark souls were attracted to the radiant glow lingering on anyone who'd recently visited the other side (like me). My grandmother had warned that until my glow faded, Dark Lifers would try to feed on this energy by touching me, drawn to the luminescence like vampires to blood.

Shivers crawled across my skin as I scanned every murky corner in the small room. The creepy "being watched" feeling persisted. I wouldn't be able to relax until I was sure the threat was a wrong number or sick joke. Not hard to check out—all I had to do was call back the text number.

I got down on my knees, and fished the phone out from underneath a chair … then groaned. Broken.

Now I couldn't call anyone—including Eli.

Tossing the useless phone aside, I sank on the bed, burying my face in my hands. What was I going to do?

Nothing—except wait for Eli. And I hated waiting. I mean, *really* hated waiting. To conquer this embarrassing character flaw I'd read a self-help book called *Paving the Road to Success through Patience*. But there were footnotes and the advice was so boring that I ended up skimming through the chapters, learning only that I really sucked at being patient.

Obviously I sucked at being a Temp Lifer, too. My first act on the job was to break Sharayah's cell phone—how pathetic was that? And instead of coming up with a plan of action, I was waiting to be rescued by her brother. But what else could I do? Being in someone else's body without knowing much about them was like driving to an unknown destination blindfolded. Where could I find out more about Sharayah?

With a snap of my fingers, I turned to the two computers in the room. One was a slim, silver laptop propped on a white desk painted with elegant rose vines; the desktop was neat and organized, with metal racks for papers, pens, folders, and books. The only personal items were a pink quartz paperweight and a rhinestone-framed graduation picture of a pink-haired girl with a pierced lip. The roommate, I guessed. The other computer, a black laptop, sat on a dark wood desk, which was so cluttered that the laptop was half-hidden behind random papers, boxes, books, and CDs.

Pushing aside a folder and two textbooks, I plopped into the swivel chair and booted up Sharayah's laptop, tapping my fingers impatiently. A box popped up asking for my password. I tried combinations of Sharayah's first and last name and even her birth date (which I found in her wallet), but nothing worked. I was ready to give up when I noticed a fingerprint swipe. Was her fingerprint her password? While this was cool, it was also discouraging, because how could I fake her fingerprint?

Then I slapped my head. Well, duh. I *was* Sharayah.

Curling the fingers in on my right hand and sticking out my thumb I started to swipe my thumbprint—when there was a knock on the door.

I jerked away from the computer, frozen with panic. Who could it be, so early in the morning? Not Sharayah's roommate—she'd have a key and wouldn't bother to knock. What about the shirtless boyfriend? Could he be coming back after his shirt? Or was it the person who'd sent the threatening text? I glanced uneasily at the broken phone with its dead, dark screen.

The knocking persisted, louder and insistent. My dorm neighbors would wake up if I didn't answer. I stared at the door, biting my lip, wishing there was a peep hole so I could see who was here. Not that I'd recognize any of Sharayah's friends or enemies. I couldn't decide what to do.

"Forget waiting," I muttered.

Then I yanked open the door—and found myself face-to-face with somebody famous. I mean, a real-for-glamness Hollywood star!

She was so famous she only had one name, which was recognizable around the world, and even though she wore sweats with a baseball cap pulled low over her forehead, she looked gorgeous. What had I heard about her recently? Something about a breakdown after adopting her eighth baby and rumors that her hubby was leaving her?

"Don't just stand here," the diva snapped in the silky voice she'd used before vaporizing her lover in her last action movie. "Those vile photographers will spot me again and I'll be mobbed."

"But you're ... you're—!" My jaw sagged open.

"Don't say it! As if I haven't heard that name a million times too many in the last few days," she said with a sweep of her hand as she moved past me into the room. "I am so sick of this celebrity crap and I detest all those flashing cameras. This has got to be the worse job in the history of worst jobs. Shut that door already—unless you want to be on every trash newspaper and YouTube around the world."

I slammed the door then spun toward her. "How did you ... I mean ... um ... have we met before?"

"Not in this lifetime."

Something about her tone hinted that she was more than a movie star, which only added to my confusion. Maybe hanging out with celebrities was normal for Sharayah, but I had to push down my inner fan-girl and act cool.

"So ... um ... what's this about?" I asked.

"We'll get to that in a minute."

She whipped off her cap and shook out luxurious black hair that shimmered around her slim shoulders. Even without makeup, her beauty was stunning. I had a strong impulse to beg for her autograph.

Have some pride, I scolded myself. My self-help books advised treating everyone the same, emphasizing that just because someone was considered a "star" didn't make them more important than anyone else. Still, I found it hard to follow this advice when I was inches away from one of the most famous divas in the world.

"I hope you appreciate all the trouble I went through to get here, and don't even think about griping because I'm a teensy bit late." She turned toward the full-length mirror, puckering her glossy lips and finger-combing her hair. "Gawd, I'm a mess. Circles under my eyes, and is that a wrinkle? And I didn't get any sleep tonight thanks to this assignment."

"Assignment?" I echoed.

She gave me a look like I was the stupidest person she'd ever met. "Why else would I come all the way here, this early? This was the only time I could slip away without being followed. Do you have any idea how exhausting it is to be famous?"

Actually I could imagine, since I'd read dozens of movie and music star's autobiographies to prepare for my future career managing Hollywood careers. But I didn't think that's what she wanted to hear, so I just shrugged.

"Of course you don't know—no one can unless they live in this body." She waved her bejeweled hand at me dismissively. "Running lines, hours in a makeup chair, shooting the same scene a million times, fans sucking up to me like leaches, but the worse is being hounded by rabid paparazzi. Can you believe I drove all the way here before discovering this psycho photographer hiding in my trunk? The idiot couldn't get out and his banging was giving me a headache. I'm sure someone will eventually let him out." She rubbed her forehead, then held out a paper to me. "This is for you, Amber."

"Amber?" I grabbed hold of a dresser so I didn't fall over from shock. "You know my name?"

"Hel-lo?" She rolled her glamorous eyes. "Haven't you been listening to anything I've said? Why else would I come here at this gawd-awful time with your delivery? All right, so I should have been here right after your switch, I suppose I should apologize, but getting anywhere in this high-mainte-nance body isn't easy."

"Body? You mean ... you're a Temp Lifer like me?"

"A Temp Lifer—yes. But an untrained novice like you? No. I have a hundred and forty-three years of experience and

I had the wisdom not to volunteer until after I'd been dead a few decades. I don't approve of using Earthbounders as TLs, but no one asked for my opinion and it doesn't happen often anyway, usually only when someone pulls harp strings up there." She pointed upward with a disapproving sniff. "But I suppose nepotism is everywhere."

"I didn't ask for this job!" I snapped. "It's horrible not being myself and being trapped in someone else's body—especially this one! I just want to go home and be myself again."

"So why'd you volunteer?"

"It was an accident. I didn't know what I was promising when I told my grandmother I'd help out. And I certainly didn't think she'd switch me right away—but everything happened so fast. I had no idea she'd do this to me without a warning, or at least some instructions. This is the worst thing to happen in my whole life—and considering I was hit by a truck and nearly died last week, that's saying a lot. I just want to go back to my own body. This is so unfair."

"How about getting over yourself?" She tucked her luxurious locks back under the cap. "And while you're doing that, sign this form so I can get out of here."

"Didn't you hear anything I said? I don't want to be a Temp Lifer."

"There's no quitting on the other side," she said with a small shrug. "You want out? Complete your assignment—which means signing this paper."

"I refuse to sign anything without reading it first."

"So read it—but be quick."

I squinted at the small print and legalese. "Um ... should

I get a lawyer? This is hard to understand. For all I know I'm signing away my soul."

"Trust me—you'd know if you were," she said ominously. "Soul signing is serious business and only binding when using blood ink."

"Blood ink? Gross. I am so not cut out for this job." I groaned. "Can you get a message to my grandmother and ask her to replace me with someone more experienced? I don't have any idea what to do. I know whose body I'm in, but I don't know what her problem is and or how to solve it."

"You're such a newbie. The TL job is to replace, not rescue. We give our Host Soul a rest so they can come back refreshed enough to solve their own problems. But you wouldn't know that, since this is only your first experience in a different body."

Her condescending tone made me bristle. "Actually, it's my second." I didn't add that the first time had been a cosmic accident caused by my pathetic sense of direction and I hadn't known what to do then, either.

"Seriously?" She arched a skeptic brow. "You've done this before?"

"I … um … helped a girl at school who tried to commit suicide."

"They trusted a suicide to a novice? What are the other worlds coming to? Oh well, not my problem. Would you sign already?" She snapped her fingers and suddenly a feather-tipped pen appeared in her hand. She shoved it at me. "Once you read and sign the release form, I'll give you your Guidance Evaluation Manual—or GEM as we call them—which will tell you everything you need to know. Then I'm so out of here. I can only hope my next assignment is somewhere far from Hollywood and more peaceful—like a war zone."

Holding the pen between my fingers, I read the small print.

> *As the undersigned Temporary Lifer, I agree to abide by all existing and future rules incorporated in the Guidance Evaluation Manual and agree herewith to offer no allegations against the High Power and all its agencies ... blah, blah, blah.*

My grandmother must know a lot of lawyers on the other side, I thought as I skipped down to the part of the page where I signed my life away—an act I hoped wasn't a bad pun.

"Great." The diva snatched the paper and folded it over and over until it was so small that it vanished in her hand. A snap of her fingers and a book appeared, if you could call something no bigger than a Hershey's bar a book. She shoved it at me. "Study this GEM and do not—I mean *do not under any circumstances*—break the rules."

I nodded, a little uneasy but mostly curious as I palmed the tiny book. When I glanced back up, eager to ask about Grammy, Sharayah, and the many other questions troubling me, the diva was gone.

For a bewildered moment I just stood there, reeling with disappointment. Then, with a sigh, I went over to Sharayah's desk to study the little book. The gold cover was blank except for three glittery letters: G-E-M. And when I flipped through the pages, they were all blank. But as I stared, a spot of black, like the tip of a pen, swirled at the center of a page, then curled into wavy lines to create a letter—*A*. Fascinated, I watched four more letters spell out *A-M-B-E-R*.

Talk about personalizing a book! Now the letters came faster, spilling like a vein of ink had been opened, pouring words onto the page to compose a short letter to me.

Amber,

Your role as a Temp Lifer is vital to your Host Soul as well as a beacon of redemption for all negativity and mistakes along your personal life path. Earthbounders require care and upkeep when they are in trauma mode. During the soul replacement, you will assume the Host Soul's life with no interruptions. Your signature has been noted in the Hall of Records as your binding promise to abide by all regulations and obligations of this sacred mission. Adhere to each of the Nine Divine Rules; breaking any Rule could result in serious consequences.

The ink paused, and the page fluttered to a new page that was no longer empty. It included a single line: *Nine Divine Rules.*

The page flipped again to show the first rule.

> *#1. Follow through on your Host Body's obligations and plans.*

It would help to know Sharayah's plans, I thought as the page flipped quickly to the next rule.

> *#2. Under no circumstances should you ever reveal your true identity.*

Oops, blew that one already by telling Eli, I thought, with a glance at the broken phone. Less than an hour as a Temp Lifer and I'd already broken a rule. I hoped Grammy wouldn't be mad.

The pages flipped faster now. I had to read quickly so I wouldn't miss important information.

#3. Consult this manual with pertinent questions.

#4. Resist temptation; guide your Host to positive choices.

#5. If you become aware of Dark Lifers, retreat and report.

#6. Do not commit acts against your Host's moral code.

#7. Respect your Host Body; no tattoos, hair dye, or piercings.

#8. Your time in a Host Body cannot exceed a full moon cycle.

#9. Guard your Host Body well. If your Body dies, so will you.

I reread the ninth rule a few times, my stomach knotting. Why make a rule like that unless it had actually happened? Had an unfortunate Temp Lifer died on the job and lost their real body as a penalty? Talk about on-the-job hazards! Taking over someone else's life was way too dangerous. I wished I'd never made that stupid promise to Grammy. Did she know I'd already broken the second rule? Not that it was my fault, because I hadn't even known about the rules when I'd called Eli. And to be honest, I didn't regret breaking that rule. Even if I'd known it was forbidden, I probably would have called Eli. He deserved to know about his sister.

Still, rule-breaking made me uneasy ... guilty. From now on, no matter what, I wouldn't break any more rules. Whether I wanted this job or not, Eli, my grandmother and Sharayah were counting on me—and I couldn't let them down.

I started to close the book when pages flipped as if caught up in a sudden wind, revealing a page with the most puzzling message yet:

Inquire here with pertinent questions regarding your Host Body.

Huh? What did that mean? How was I suppose to "inquire" and where exactly was "here"? I stared, waiting for further instructions, but there weren't any. And when I flipped back to the beginning, everything I'd already read had vanished.

"Grammy," I grumbled with a gaze up toward the semi-dark ceiling, "why are you making this so hard?"

Holding my breath, I half-expected to hear her reply, but all I heard was the increasing thump of my own heartbeat. And when I looked back down at the book, bold black ink spewed into words.

Your mission is only as hard as you make it.

I squinted down at the book, afraid that if I blinked these words would vanish, too. Then I must have blinked, because the page was empty again. But I was beginning to understand a little. This candy-bar-sized book was my connection to the other side.

"How am I supposed to help Sharayah?" I asked it.

Refer to Rule One.

"But the rules aren't written down any more!" I argued.

#1. Follow through on your Host Body's obligations and plans.

"Sarcastic book, aren't you?"

The page cleared itself of ink again—which was answer enough.

"Okay, this is starting to make sense. I ask you a question and you give me an answer. Will you tell me anything I ask?"

The book cover slammed shut.

"I take that as a no," I said, frowning. "Can you at least tell me about Sharayah's crisis? Does it have to do with the boyfriend Gabe, college, or all that money?"

I waited for an answer, the book cupped in my hands, only there was no flutter of reply.

"Come on," I urged. "Open up again and write to me. I need to know about Sharayah's problems. What am I supposed to do for her?"

The book flopped open and one word scrawled on the page.

Live.

Now that really told me a big fat page of nothing. I already knew I was supposed to live her life, at least temporarily. But did that mean I was supposed to sit around this dorm room until my temp time was up? Or did Sharayah have obligations like a job or homework? I didn't want to hang around accomplishing nothing—I wanted to be Super Amber and solve all problems.

Okay, okay … so maybe solving problems might not technically be my job. But Sharayah obviously needed help or she wouldn't have cut off her family and dumped her former roommate/best friend. There was also the money and the text threat. Why would Grammy say I was good at helping people if that's not what she wanted me to do? And she must have had a good reason for choosing me for this mission. My knowing Eli couldn't be the reason, because that was just awkward and complicated my assignment. So why choose me instead of an experienced Temp Lifer? Did I have a unique ability or talent that made me a good match for this job? I couldn't think of anything.

I glanced at the clock, wondering if Eli was on his way. Even if he'd gotten a car immediately, the drive would take him at least two hours. I yawned, so exhausted and overwhelmed I could hardly think straight. A short rest would feel great. And when I awoke, Eli might be here.

Tossing the GEM into the black purse, I dug a pillow from a pile of clothes on the floor then curled up on Sharayah's bed. Yawning again, I closed my eyes and slipped away into dreams.

Memories spun in kaleidoscope fragments, sweeping me back home to my family. In my living room, my little triplet sister Olive toddled after our cat Snowy, who leapt on a high shelf and transformed into a dog with a glowing collar—my (dead) dog Cola. Suddenly I was in a hospital with white walls and speckled linoleum floors, and Cola was running away. I had to catch him so he would take me to my grandmother, only he ran so fast, turning corners in a dizzy blur. I was racing on a treadmill, going nowhere. I thought I was alone until I glanced over my shoulder and saw a security guard with glowing gray hands—a Dark Lifer! He was coming closer, closer, his footsteps thudding with menace as shimmering gray fingers reached out and—

Suddenly my eyes jerked open.

I was instantly awake, panicked, but not because of my dream.

In the murky darkness, a shadowy figure loomed over the bed—watching me.

"Don't touch me!" I shouted, jerking upright and pulling the pillow close to my chest.

"What's your problem?" The shadow's voice was female and annoyed. "Stop freaking out."

"Stay back! Get away!"

"Rayah, it's just me. Are you having another nightmare?"

There was a soft click and the bedside lamp flashed on, so bright I was momentarily blinded. When my vision cleared, I saw short, prickly pink hair and black kohl eyes. This girl was older than me—oops, scratch that—I mean, older than my real self, about the same age of Sharayah. She wore snug black jeans, a black leather aviator jacket over a neon-pink shirt, and dangling, barbed-wire earrings.

"You're her…um…my roommate?" I asked, blinking away confusion.

"Are you high? Why else would I put up with you? It's not the first time you've woke up screaming. Was it the ocean nightmare again?"

"I can't remember."

"Like that surprises me." She chuckled, a silver stud on her tongue. "How much did you drink this time?"

"I honestly don't know."

"You are so bad. Didn't you get any sleep? I left so you could have privacy in here last night, but I expected you to sleep some, too. You owe me, by the way, because the twin bed Sadie loaned me was as hard as concrete. So get your ass out of bed."

"This early? We're going out?" I frowned, wishing I knew her name and how to act toward her. Were we best friends or just casual roommates?

"Of course we're going out! Your suitcase is already in the car. Did you fry all your brain cells?"

"I hope not," I said seriously. My head spun like I'd been whirling upside down on a roller coaster and a bitter taste sickened my mouth.

"Pull yourself together, okay? I can't believe you're not even ready—unless that's what you plan to wear. Hey, if you want to go in a shirt and thong, cool with me. Truckers will honk when they look down at our car." She pried the pillow from my clasped hands then tugged on my arm. "Hurry up, Rayah."

"I can't…" I shook off her grip. "I don't feel well enough to go anywhere."

"Just because you're hung-over doesn't mean we're dumping our spring break plans. If this is about your ocean phobia, no one will make you get into the water. And need I remind you that leaving so early was *your* idea?"

"It was?"

"Don't you remember anything?" She rolled her dark eyes. "You insisted we leave early because you were all paranoid about a stalker."

"The stalker! You know about that?"

"Well, duh. You showed me the note."

Note? I puzzled. Did that mean there had been other threats?

"Do you know who's threatening me?" I asked her.

"How would I? The note wasn't signed—besides, I think it's a joke. I'm always threatening to kill you—especially when you don't clean your half of the room or stink up the place with black herb tea. But I don't really mean it. And I doubt anyone else does, either. Whoever sent the note is just trying to freak you out."

"It's working," I said, hugging my shivery arms.

So there were at least two threats. I wanted to ask if there'd been any more but couldn't without causing suspicion. My heart pounded and I felt fear rising. I could understand why Sharayah needed a life break away from her stalker. It was risky for me, though, because I couldn't tell Sharayah's friends from her enemies.

"Come on, Rayah, it's already way later than we planned to leave and I'm starting to get pissed," she added accusingly. "Don't push me, okay? I was nice enough to stay with Sadie last night so you could have privacy with James. Now I find you're not even ready and still wearing his shirt."

"James?" I fingered the shirt. "That guy who left this … um … my boyfriend?"

"Ha, ha. Funny, Rayah," the roommate said with a wry chuckle. "As if you're ever serious with one guy. Sadie is waiting in the parking lot. Time to hit the road."

"Road?" My stomach lurched.

"Screw your hangover, we're leaving now." She yanked me to my feet—she was surprisingly strong despite being almost a head shorter than me. "Sadie is doing the driving and you can sleep it off on the way. Let's get out of here."

"But I can't go or I'll miss seeing—" I cut off, realizing I'd said too much.

"Seeing who?" she asked icily.

"Um … it's hard to explain."

"Don't tell me this has to do with that slacker James." She folded her arms across her busty chest, narrowing her gaze as if daring me to cross her. "I warned you he was only after one thing, which he obviously got since you're wearing his shirt."

"This has nothing to do with him." I had a sudden desire to rip off the shirt and take a shower. A long, hot, deep, body-cleaning shower.

"Then who?" she asked suspiciously. "Remember our Hands-off-Exes agreement. You better not be hitting on Kyle. Even though he's a scumbag and I am so over him, it would be too weird to see you two together."

"No, no! I mean … this isn't anyone you know."

"Then he can't be very important, can he?" She smiled. "Let's go."

"I-I can't! I have to stay and wait for—"

"Forget it! No guy is messing with our plans. We're leaving now."

"But I can't go without at least leaving him a message!"

"Call him later."

"My phone is broken." I lifted the phone, shaking it so she could hear the rattle.

"Oops. I won't even ask how that happened." The roommate chuckled wickedly. "But no prob—you can use my phone."

"Thanks. Where is it?" I held out my hand.

"In the car—where we're gonna be in a few minutes." Grabbing my hand, she yanked me toward the door. "We are leaving now."

"Wait!"

"Sure, why don't we wait?" she added with an ominous arch of her brow. "Let's give your stalker plenty of time to find you. Maybe the note isn't a joke. It could be the real deal and some psycho might really want to kill you."

"Kill me?" I gulped.

"A note that says 'I'll watch you die' isn't exactly a love letter. But you must be braver than me. I can't stop you if you'd rather wait around for your stalker than enjoy a fabulous vacation with your girlfriends."

"Okay, I'll go—but not wearing this." It was hard to think clearly; all that was clear was fear. "I'll change fast."

"I bet you will." Her smile was smug.

It was embarrassing to sway as I tried to walk, then stumbled around searching through three drawers before I found jeans that looked too long but fit great. Then I grabbed the first shirt I saw, something blue and long-sleeved. Relieved to take off the offensive James shirt, I tossed it aside and slipped into the blue top.

If only it were as easy to change out of this body and back to my own. Being my boyfriend's sister was bad enough—but being a target of a psycho terrified me. I couldn't exit the room fast enough. We made it down the hall and around a corner before I realized I didn't have Sharayah's purse—which held her ID, credit cards and the thick wad of cash.

"Oops! My purse!" I started to make a U-turn until Sharayah's roommate gave me an icy look that stopped me cold.

"Stay right here," she ordered. "I'll get it."

Reluctantly, I waited, glancing around nervously as if a stalker might pop out from a corner. I oozed relief when I saw pink hair and black leather.

She shoved the purse at me, then led me toward a set of stairs. I realized I was forgiven when she hooked her arm into mine and actually smiled. It was amazing how a simple smile made her face shine with a beauty I hadn't noticed until now.

"Venice Beach, here we come," she rang out cheerfully. "If there's time, we might even hop over the border for some serious partying in Mexico."

"Venice Beach? Mexico?" I repeated.

"That's all we'll manage in a week, although I'd love to hit Lake Havasu, too. I've always wanted to try some of that boat-to-boat partying," she announced with a jazzy dance move. "Bring on the beach, booze and badass dudes—spring break begins now!"

Her tone was upbeat but underlined with a warning not to cause any problems, and I didn't want to cross her anymore than I wanted to hang around and risk an attack from a stalker. Besides, if I didn't go with her, I'd break GEM rule #1.

1. *Follow through on your Host Body's obligations and plans.*

Apparently, one of my obligations was a vacation of partying.

Sorry, Eli, I thought. I'll call you later.

Then I left for spring break.

✱

I followed Sharayah's roommate (what was her name anyway?) down a steep stairway, then through a maze of dimly lit halls to double glass doors that led outside to the parking lot. I couldn't shake the feeling that I was being watched and kept looking around, but never saw anyone. Still, my uneasiness lingered.

It was foggy out and eerie lamps glowing like demon eyes around the parking lot added a gloomy theme to my personal nightmare. As we moved through rows of vehicles, their hulky shapes reminded me of crouching monsters. I shivered, wrapping my arms around a too-tall body that was so thin I could feel my ribs.

I peered back at the shadowy dorm I'd just left; three stories of bricked housing surrounded by shrubs and walkways. It looked traditional yet modern, the kind of dorm I hoped to attend someday with my best friend. Alyce and I had toured half a dozen campuses together, dreaming about what we'd do once we graduated from high school to real life: share a dorm room, study together, and score prestigious internships. Alyce had a trust fund and (grades permitting) she could pick and choose her college. But until recently I doubted I'd even be able to afford night classes due to my family's lack of finances, and I envisioned a future of flipping burgers at some dead-end job. Then a miracle had happened—I was offered a scholarship to a college of my choice.

But being here wasn't my choice. This was not how I imagined college life, isolated without my real friends and stumbling around in the wrong body. The simple act of walking felt all wrong, my strides so jerky that when I stumbled, only a quick grab on a rail saved me from a nasty fall. Fortunately my roommate didn't notice, or else assumed I was too wasted to walk straight...and maybe I was.

"What took you so long?" a petite girl with shiny jewels woven in her long brown braid asked, stepping away from the silver SUV she'd been leaning against. Gold bracelets jangled from her tiny wrists and she wore a designer chiffon blouse with a midnight-blue miniskirt and knee-high black boots.

"Not my fault, Sadie. Blame Rayah." The pink-haired roommate pointed an accusing finger at me. "She wasn't dressed, then she whined that she had to wait for some new guy and just when we were finally out of the room, she wanted to go back for her purse."

"How could you forget your purse?" The other girl, Sadie, looked at me like I'd committed a felony. "I don't care how wasted I am, I'd never ever leave my purse."

"I have it now." I gripped the leather bag tightly, reassured to have this small connection to my new identity even though all the cash inside made me nervous. But that was the least of my worries. I had to contact Eli or think of a way to stall long enough for him to show up.

"I still need a phone." I turned to the pink-haired girl. "You said I could use yours."

She opened the back seat door and gestured for me to get inside. "Let's wait till we're on our way."

"But it's urgent. He doesn't know I'm—"

"Don't care. Don't want to hear it." The roommate shook her head. "All you've been doing is delaying and making excuses. You're acting like some guy is more important than your best friends and this trip we've been planning for weeks."

"I never meant that."

"Then forget the guy for a while."

Sadie glanced curiously at us. Her sharp features reminded me of a bird: not an ordinary sparrow, but a bright and exotic macaw, shining with shades of sapphire, cinnamon and sunset red. "Aren't you being harsh, Mauve?" she asked the pink-haired girl. "If Rayah wants to call some dude, what's the harm? Don't be such a bitch."

"Why not? I am one and proud of it."

"Yeah—I saw it on a bumper sticker. *Mauve: Campus Bitch.*"

Mauve snorted. "You think you're so funny."

"Someone around here has to be." Sadie's car keys jangled as she slipped into the driver's seat. "So who's the new guy, Rayah?"

"Oh, it's not like that!" I felt my face reddening. "I mean, he's more like … um … a brother. But it's important I call him … can I borrow your phone?"

"Don't give it to her until we're on the freeway and there's

33

no turning back, Sadie," Mauve interrupted with an accusing look at me as she opened the door to the passenger side of the front seat. "She's been acting all kinds of weird. I don't know what's going on, but it's more than a hangover. Rayah, is there something you're not telling us?"

"Of course not."

"Then get into the car."

"Fine. Whatever." I scooted into the back seat.

Sadie glanced at Mauve and then me with pinched lips. "You know what we need?"

"A phone," I said.

"A new roommate," Mauve said.

"Wrong." With a big smile, Sadie slid into the car and reached for a bag. "Mocha lattes. Since you were taking so long, I ran over to Starbucks and got our usual."

I inhaled a rich scent of coffee as I took the hot cup and pulled off the lid. But when I took a sip, I nearly spit it out. Whoa! Sharayah's "usual" was strong enough to sober up a career drunk. I rarely drank coffee, and when I did I dumped in loads of cream and sugar. Stealthily, I put the lid back on and squeezed the cup into a holder.

"That should cure Rayah's hangover. She really tied one on with *James*." Mauve spoke his name in a mocking way. "When I got to the room, she was wearing his shirt."

"And the partying begins," Sadie said cheerfully as she fastened her seat belt. "Between you two, my Layaway List is growing fast. How would you rate James? Was he any good? Details, please."

"Um … well … " I blushed, having no idea how to answer this.

"That bad, huh? Next time you can teach him a few of your tricks." Sadie said this in a tone that implied I had plenty of experience with guys.

My cheeks flamed and I was glad to be sitting in the back where they couldn't see my face. In my real body, I'd kissed a total of four guys and had never gone farther than second base. I was so *not* experienced—definitely not enough to score anyone or teach them "tricks." And I was pretty sure Sadie's "Layaway List" had nothing to do with shopping for clothes at the mall.

Mentally, I started my own list of People to Avoid:

#1. James.
#2. The Stalker.

Posing as Sharayah might be easier away from the dorm. It was hard enough to fool Mauve and Sadie, but if I stayed on campus I'd run into more people who knew more about me than I knew about myself—which would be all kinds of awkward.

Still, leaving meant not seeing Eli. But maybe I could meet up with him later—if I could ever call him. Mauve continued to be a bitch about using her phone and warned Sadie not to loan me hers, either.

I needed a plan to delay leaving until Eli showed up. Anxiety made me nauseous, and I gripped my stomach … and then smiled.

Being sick—perfect!

"Oooh," I groaned with exaggerated drama.

Sadie whirled around to face me. "Rayah, you okay?"

"Ignore her and start the car," Mauve snapped.

"I'm not feeling … ooh!" I covered my mouth and sagged forward.

"Drink your latte," Mauve said. "That'll sober you up."

I shook my head, adding gagging sounds to my groans.

"Rayah, hold yourself together," Sadie begged. "Don't you dare hurl in my car!"

The weird thing was that once I thought about my stomach, I really did feel sick. Bile burned my throat. When I doubled over, moaning, I wasn't faking it. My insides rebelled, roiling and pitching like a storm. Oh, no ... no! I unfastened my seat belt, yanked open the door, and spewed on the pavement.

When I was able to lift my head I felt lighter and much, much better. I gulped in damp foggy air and avoided looking at the ground by glancing around the parking lot. A flash of light caught my attention in the opposite row of cars. An interior light glowed from a dark-colored compact car, spotlighting a girl in the driver's seat with curly red hair and pale skin. Her gaze was fixed my way and she was staring directly—furiously—at me. Then the illumination faded, dimming slowly until the girl seemed to vanish in the fog.

But those angry eyes continued to burn in my memory, and while I didn't personally know the redheaded girl, I was positive she knew—and hated—Sharayah.

"**A**re you done yet?" Mauve asked, stepping out of the car. She walked over, then glanced down at the ground and made a bitter face. "Eww, that's so gross."

"Sorry." I wobbled back into the car on rubbery legs and snapped my seat belt back on. "I've never done anything like that before."

"Ha!" Mauve snorted. "Try telling that to someone who hasn't roomed with you for three months. But hey, it's all in fun."

Fun? Getting sick and spewing in a parking lot was *fun*? Did Mauve really mean that or was she being sarcastic again? It was impossible to tell with Mauve (was that her real name, anyway, or an accessory to match her hair?). Her sarcasm didn't faze me, though, not like the hatred from the red-haired girl. Who was she and what did she have against Sharayah? If facial expressions came with subtitles, hers would have read, "Die a painful death right now so I can laugh while you suffer."

I couldn't get her twisted fury out of my head, and there was also this gnawing feeling … an odd sense of recognition, as if something inside my borrowed body remembered her with emotions of bitterness, fear, and guilt.

Sadie started the car, its headlights sweeping across the parking lot. I peered through the misty light for the girl but saw only reflections of headlights glaring back at me.

"Did you see that girl?" I tapped Sadie's shoulder as the car shifted with a lurch into reverse. "Hiding in a car?"

"What girl?" Sadie asked, glancing at me in the rearview mirror.

"Over there—in that row." I pointed. "She had curly red hair and was just sitting alone in one of those cars. Did either of you see her?"

"All I saw was my roommate puking," Mauve said.

Sadie looked around curiously. "Which car?"

"That car … or maybe that one … " Murky shapes blended together. "I'm not sure anymore."

"Well, duh," Mauve said dryly. "You're so wasted you're hallucinating."

"No, I'm feeling fine now and know what I saw. A mid-sized car, either brown or black, and there was this girl with red hair glaring at me like she wanted me dead. Do you know of a girl that hates me?"

"*A* girl? You've pissed off so many girls they probably have a club." Mauve chuckled. "You won't win any popularity awards around here—at least with the girlfriends of guys you hit on."

"You don't want to be boring and self-righteous like them anyway," Sadie said.

"Especially Katelyn Myers," Mauve added. "She really hates you."

"No big loss." Sadie settled back into the driver's seat, catching my gaze in the rearview mirror. "Katelyn thinks she's all that 'cause she won a beauty pageant. The way she goes around showing off her tiara makes me want to, well, what you just did. It's not even a real title—she was Miss Pickle Barrel, which is definitely something I wouldn't brag about if I were her."

We left the parking lot and as I replayed the red-haired-girl incident in my head, I decided it was random, not personal. If I saw someone puking in the parking lot, I'd be disgusted and might glare at them, too. That didn't mean the girl had any malicious intent against me. Blame my paranoia or being overtired and overwhelmed. People who sent threats were cowards and rarely had the guts to actually follow through. Sharayah wasn't in real danger—except from her self-destructive behavior. I dreaded telling Eli what I'd found out about his sister.

But there was no rush to tell him. I'd wait until I figured out a way to solve Sharayah's problems. If everything worked out and Sharayah started seeing her family again, Eli would be really grateful to me. We'd finally go out on our first real date. He'd bring me flowers and I'd surprise him with a box of chocolates—which we'd share. I was envisioning a romantic future with Eli as I leaned my head against the seat, having no plans to close my eyes or go to sleep.

But I did anyway.

When I woke up, the fog had burned off and we were stopped in traffic under a glaring sun. Not the kind of traffic that crawled slowly, bumper to bumper, but the kind where you're jammed in on every side by an infinite string of cars with no hope of getting anywhere. The CD in our car blared rap so loudly that my head throbbed, and underneath the noise I heard swearing.

"This sucks! It'll be tomorrow before we get to the beach. This is more like a parking lot than a freeway! What's with all these cars? Damn!" Mauve waved her fist as if the traffic was a personal insult against her.

"I saw a sign warning about road construction," Sadie said, "but I never expected it to be this bad."

"Stupid construction! If this traffic doesn't move soon, we'll die here of old age." Mauve reached across the front seat to smack the horn, which accomplished nothing except pissing off other drivers who honked their horns. My head hurt.

"I can't believe I slept for so long!" I groaned. "Where are we anyway?"

"Somewhere between Bakersfield and hell," Mauve grumbled, catching my gaze in the rearview mirror. "I thought we'd avoid traffic by leaving early."

I leaned forward to check the clock on the dashboard, and nearly flipped out. I'd been asleep for over three hours— which meant we'd driven nearly two hundred miles away from the dorm. Away from Eli.

Leaning over to Mauve, I held out my hand. "I need your phone!"

"Huh?" Mauve flipped her pink hair from her eyes and turned toward me as if she'd forgotten I existed.

"Your phone. Now!"

"Oh, sure. Why didn't you ask sooner?" Mauve turned around with her hand extended toward me. "Who you calling?"

"Um … a friend."

"I bet I know." Sadie glanced over the seat at me, grinning knowingly. "James."

Mauve raised her brows, but didn't ask any questions as I took the pink-cased flip phone. Quickly, I tapped in the number. Numbers I was good with—but having a boyfriend was still new to me, and obviously I sucked at it as badly as I did at being a Temp Lifer. I hoped Eli wasn't too mad about being stood up.

Eli picked up on the third ring. "Hello?" His tone sounded puzzled, as if he was staring at the phone screen trying to figure out who was calling.

I wanted to say so many things, but even with the CD playing I suspected my companions would overhear, so I just whispered, "It's me."

"Sharay … um … Amber?"

"You got it on the second guess."

"Amber!" He exclaimed with both relief and anger. "Where the hell are you?"

"Somewhere on I-5 headed south." I looked out the window at a sea of stalled traffic wedged in by rocky, weed-spotted hills with an occasional flat oasis of emerald green fields.

"You're WHERE?! Why didn't you wait for me at the college?" His voice exploded through the phone so loudly that Mauve heard it over her the rap music and turned around with a questioning gaze. I shrugged with my arms out as if to gesture that dealing with irate guys was no big deal.

But it was a big deal to me and I felt awful.

"I'm so sorry, E—" I almost spoke his name until I caught myself and lowered my voice. "Everything happened fast and I couldn't figure a way out."

"Ever think of saying no?" he demanded. "I freaking can't believe this."

"Me, either." My seat belt tugged at my waist as I slumped in my seat. "I can't really explain now."

"It's been four hours and twenty-five minutes since I heard from you," he calculated in that savvy math-geek way that had attracted me to him in the first place. "What took you so long to call?"

"Um…this body had a rough night…I kind of fell asleep."

There was silence for a minute, then I heard his sigh. "I'm trying to stay cool about all of this, but do you have any idea what I thought when I couldn't get you on the phone or find you at the dorm?"

I winced with guilt. "No."

"Well first I had to prove to the residential assistant that I was Sharayah's brother before she even let me in the dorm. She escorted me to your—I mean, Sharayah's—room. We knocked but no one was there."

"We'd already left."

"Obviously—but I didn't know that and I thought you

might be in trouble, so I insisted the R.A. open the door. She was already pissed at my showing up so early but seemed worried, too, so she used her key to open the door. When I saw how trashed the room was and found the broken phone, I was ready to call 911. But this girl from across the hall, Katelyn, came over and said that's how the room usually looks."

"Your sister is a slob," I agreed.

"She didn't used to be—but then, she didn't used to be a lot of things," he said sadly. "Katelyn told me she'd heard you and your roommate leaving about an hour earlier. She didn't seem to like my sister very much."

"I've heard," I said wryly. "So where are you now?"

He didn't answer, and I thought the phone had disconnected until I heard him clear his throat. "Um ... well, I couldn't leave without finding you and the resident manager wouldn't let me wait in the room for legal reasons because only half of the room belongs to my sister. I didn't know whether to leave or wait for you to come back. But then Katelyn offered to let me wait in her room, so that's where I am."

"In *her* room?"

"It was either there or my car."

"I choose your car."

"Where else was I supposed to go? You didn't even leave me a note."

"I didn't get a chance." I tried to sound calm and not let on that I wanted to rip out Katelyn's hair. I wasn't jealous. Not me. "So are you still with the bi ... I mean, Katelyn?"

"I'm in her room but she's not here."

"Where is she?"

"In the shower."

"Shower!" My voice rose so loudly that Sadie and Mauve turned to stare at me.

"Who's getting naked?" Sadie giggled.

"At least someone's having fun," Mauve said with a pouty scowl.

I covered the mouthpiece with my hand and told them, "It's not like that. My friend is describing how to fix a shower drain." I added an exaggerated eye roll like I was bored out of my mind, hoping they would lose interest and turn around.

They finally did—but not because of anything I said. A red convertible in the next lane caught Mauve's attention and she whipped around to point. "Check it out!" she shouted, "Hot guys!"

While Mauve rolled her window down, I returned my attention to Eli who was saying, "—shower is way down the hall. But even if it was in the same room, what does it matter? Are you jealous?"

"No way," I lied.

"Sure about that?"

"Positive," I retorted. "But you don't need to stay there anymore."

"I know, I'm coming to get you," Eli offered. "Where are you headed?"

"A condo in Venice Beach," I told him, my gaze drifting over to Mauve, who was half-hanging out the window waving at the guys in the next lane.

"It'll take me hours to drive that far. Wait at a rest stop or business and I'll pick you up. Tell your friends you need to go home because of a family emergency."

"I can't change plans now." I dropped my voice to a whisper. "I'm supposed to follow through on your sister's plans. And I'm safer away from the dorm, anyway."

"Safer? What are you talking about?"

"Sharayah has been getting threats, although they could be a joke."

"Threats? What kind of mess has my sister gotten into?" Eli groaned. "Any idea who sent them?"

I hesitated, thinking of the red-haired girl. "Not really."

"Damn. Why didn't Sharayah tell us? I feel like I've let her down."

"It's not your fault."

"Be careful, and stick close to Shari's friends."

I looked over at Mauve and Sadie, who were both hanging out their separate windows as they flirted with the guys in the convertible.

"Tops up!" Mauve called over to Sadie.

"On the count of three!" Sadie giggled.

"One, two—" Mauve began.

"Three!" Sadie finished.

They flipped up their tops and flashed the guys. It happened so fast that all I caught was a flash of arms lifting and flesh. Nudity on Interstate Five!

"—don't go anywhere alone," Eli was saying.

"No such luck," I said ruefully.

"It's a good thing you left the college. You'll be safer around my sister's friends."

Safer—assuming my companions didn't get arrested for indecent exposure!

Shaking my head, I turned away from the road show and

assured Eli I'd be fine. "But things will be easier once I consult with my GEM."

"GEM? What's that?"

"A Temp Lifer guidance manual." I spoke so softly I could hardly hear myself. "If I ask the book a question, it'll tell me stuff about my mission."

"Your grandmother gave you a manual? Great! When did you see her?"

"I didn't actually see her." I hesitated, wondering how much weirdness Eli could take. "The book was delivered by … you won't believe it."

"Try me."

I swallowed, then glanced up to make sure Mauve and Sadie couldn't overhear (they were now whistling cat calls at the "Hot Guys"), then blurted out the famous name.

He gasped. "You talked with her?"

"It wasn't really her. She was replaced with a Temp Lifer like me—except, well, this TL has been doing this for way longer."

"Did you get her autograph?"

"How can you even ask such a question?" I tried to sound insulted so he wouldn't guess how close I came to doing just that. "Celebrities don't impress me. They're just ordinary people like us."

"Ordinary—you are definitely not."

"Tell me about it." I groaned as I glanced down at my borrowed body. "But at least the GEM will help."

"Shari seriously needs help. Can your book explain why she changed so much and why someone's stalking her?"

"I'll ask," I said, reaching for Sharayah's purse.

Laughter erupted from the front seat. I glanced up as

Mauve flung open her door and gestured toward the two guys in the red convertible. Wasn't flashing them bad enough? Now she was inviting them over! I looked at Sadie, hoping she'd have some common sense, but she had her door open, too, and was waving eagerly at the guys.

Pure insanity! Those guys could be perverts or ex-convicts or even married. I'd never behave so irresponsibly...but what about the real Sharayah? I had a bad feeling she would have flashed, too—but not because she enjoyed being a player. Her body sent me simmering undercurrents of anger and guilt. No, she didn't party to have a good time; she partied to punish herself.

I hoped the GEM would help me solve her crisis.

Tucking the phone between my ear and shoulder, I reached inside the purse—but didn't feel the squared edges of a book. Puzzled, I dumped the purse out. A wallet, keys, makeup and other items fell in my lap.

No gold-covered book.

My body went hot, then cold, and then scorching hot as my thoughts raced back to when I'd last seen the GEM. I was in the dorm, sick with nausea and so exhausted I couldn't stay awake. I was positive I'd tossed the GEM into Sharayah's purse. I'd heard a soft thud as it hit the purse. But did I check to make sure it fell inside? Um...nope.

"Amber! Are you there?" I heard Eli calling. "Say something."

"I don't have the GEM." I stared dismally out a window, reeling in disappointment. That tiny book had been my only connection to the other side—and I'd lost it.

"Do you know where it is?" Eli asked.

"It must be in the dorm room."

"I'd go look for it, except the door is locked and I doubt the R.A. will let me in again," Eli said. "I could ask Katelyn to help—"

"No! Don't ask her!"

"What do you expect me to do?" he retorted. "Break into your room?"

"Would you?" I asked, half-seriously.

"Sure, I've always wanted to get arrested."

"Well ... I guess it's not such a good idea."

Still, I couldn't just give up on the GEM, not when it held the answers to Sharayah's crisis. I'd recently had some experience getting in and out of locked rooms and even a locked cemetery—but I hadn't done it on my own. I'd had the help of friends.

This gave me an idea.

"Listen," I told Eli in an urgent whisper. "If you're serious about getting the book, call Dustin."

"Why?"

I was reminding him about Dustin's locksmith expertise and his amazing collection of keys when a blur of pink hair swooped around from the front seat and snatched the phone right out of my hand.

"No more talking, Rayah!" Mauve ordered.

"Hey!" I shouted, glaring at her. "Give that back!"

"Come on! Why are you talking to *him* when there are guys everywhere?"

"But I wasn't finished."

"Now you are." Mauve snapped the phone shut. "Traffic may not be making moves, but I am. Here come the guys!"

Picking up guys in traffic was insane—not to mention embarrassing. I wanted to hide while Mauve and Sadie flaunted their assets. Mauve's grin was jubilant, like finding guys was a contest and she'd won top prize. She stepped out of the car and exchanged introductions.

The big guy, Warren, towered over everyone with his linebacker shoulders and snow-blond hair. His black, short-sleeved shirt opened over a red T-shirt dripping with a fiery dragon design that matched the design on his red leather gloves. Gloves? I thought, surprised. That style went out with Michael Jackson.

At least the other guy, Alonzo, seemed normal—and extremely cute, with a tight body, springy black curls and soft, full lips. From the way Mauve was eyeing him, it was obvious she'd staked her claim.

"Yo, girls," Warren said with the eloquence of a cave man. "How ya' doing?"

"Much better now," Sadie said as she sidled up to him.

"Yeah," Mauve agreed, her gaze lingering on cute Alonzo. "The traffic is insane but I don't mind so much now."

They were paired up evenly and didn't need me. So I said nothing, having zero flirting style. I tried to blend invisibly into the seat, humming to the CD. But of course I was listening to the drama unfolding outside with acute fascination.

"So, hey," Alonzo flipped his black curls in Mauve's direction. "Where you headed?"

"Venice," Mauve answered.

"Italy?" Warren said with a snort, like he'd made a joke.

"You're too funny," Sadie giggled.

Gag me. Sadie couldn't really like this brute, could she?

At least Mauve wasn't impressed with Warren. She rolled her eyes. "Venice *Beach*," she corrected him.

"For spring break?"

"What else?" Mauve leaned against the open car door and turned to Alonzo with a bright smile. "So how about you?"

"Same, except Warren and I keep our options open so we got no definite plans. You really know how to get a guy's attention, although I would have noticed you anywhere," Alonzo said, reaching over and curling a strand of her spiky hair around his finger.

"Hey, Lonz, check out the back seat." Warren suddenly peered through Mauve's open window and leaned over to wave at me. "There's another girl."

"That's Rayah," Sadie chirped. "She had a wild night and spewed in a parking lot this morning. She's kind of out of it."

"I'm just tired," I said with an exaggerated yawn, hoping Warren would get the hint and leave me alone.

But no such luck.

"Party Girl, come out and party with us," Warren urged.

"You go ahead without me."

"Come on, Warren, let Rayah rest." Sadie moved closer to Warren, obviously realizing that two guys divided by three girls weren't great odds unless you removed one girl from the equation.

Warren ignored her and tapped on my window. "Come on, join our road party. You'll have more fun with us."

"I'm enjoying the music," I said, pointing to the front seat where Sadie had kept the power on and music playing. I bobbed my head to the rhythm to show I was having plenty of fun sitting by myself.

"If it's music you want to hear, Lonz and I have some cool CDs in our car."

What was it with this guy? Sadie was practically dripping all over him yet he wouldn't leave me alone. So I shook my head in a firm *no*.

"Forget her, I'd love to hear your CDs," Sadie told Warren. "Let's go to your car."

"And leave your friend?" Warren stared me in a way that gave me shivers.

"If you know what's good for you," Mauve put in with a wicked grin. She raked her black-tipped fingernails through her pink head and gave Warren a warning look. "You better leave Rayah alone."

"Why?" he asked, frowning.

"After a night of partying, she's got a short fuse." Mauve turned so I could see her face (but the guys couldn't) and winked at me. "If you push her, she could get dangerous."

Me, dangerous? Was Mauve trying to help me or stirring up drama for her own amusement? I was like the most non-violent person ever. I rarely lost my temper—not even when my little sisters turned an essay I'd spent a week writing into paper diapers for their dolls.

Mauve's lie was ridiculous... or was it? What if Sharayah's personality change included violence? How could I be sure until I knew more about her? I needed the GEM to tell me the truth. Then I wouldn't stumble around in this borrowed body like an actress without a script.

"Let's go sit in your car," Sadie urged Warren, gently pulling on his arm.

"Sure." Warren glanced over at Alonzo. "You coming or staying here?"

"Coming, as soon as I'm done listening." He tilted his head toward the car stereo, which was still playing loud and strong. "I didn't know this album was out yet."

"It's new. I'll burn you a CD, for a price." Mauve smiled.

"A price?" Alonzo asked, grinning. "What did you have in mind?"

"What can you give me?" Mauve asked playfully.

"I can think of a lot of things—but not in public." Alonzo rubbed his thumb over his lip ring. "Maybe we should wait till this traffic clears up and go somewhere private."

"Whoa, you're moving too fast," Mauve said with a flirty laugh. "All I'm offering is a CD... for now."

"Excuse me, but that's my CD." Sadie whirled from Warren to glare at Mauve. "You can't give away my stuff."

"I'd never take anything of *yours*," Mauve said, with a hard emphasis on "yours" that abruptly shut Sadie up. Sadie pressed her lips tightly and stepped away from Mauve.

What was that about? I wondered, leaning closer so I wouldn't miss a word. I was puzzled yet intrigued, like watching a movie with subtitles.

I was relieved to watch them leave and sit anonymously in the back seat, analyzing my feelings about this "college girls gone wild" drama. Part of me was appalled by the way my "friends" were acting, yet another part was impressed. Mauve handled the guys with enough attitude to stay in control. Even over-eager Sadie carried herself with a bold confidence.

And I felt like a high school girl—for good reason.

Sharayah wouldn't be sitting nervously in the back seat like me. But without the GEM I didn't know enough about her to know what to do. What did I know about spring break? Only what I'd watched on TV.

Of course Sharayah probably didn't know much about spring break, either. According to Eli, she used to be so studious that she never had time for anything except homework and volunteering. A far cry from this new Sharayah, who partied hard, trashed her dorm room and randomly hooked up with guys. I didn't think her behavior had anything to do with drugs—I would have suffered symptoms or cravings by now. Something traumatic happened to change her. But what? Was it the older boyfriend, Gabe? Hmmm ... where was Gabe anyway? If he was "my" boyfriend, why did Mauve say Sharayah didn't have a steady guy?

Suddenly there was a roar of shouts, honks and cheers. The traffic was moving! I leaned forward to peer out the window as the others rushed back.

"Taillights are flashing!" Sadie announced, jumping excitedly.

"So soon? Too bad, I was enjoying the view." Alonzo leaned on the open door, his gaze lingering on Mauve.

"We can hook up later." Mauve smiled. "We're staying at Sadie's cousin's beach condo." She rattled off an address on Tide Pool Street, which I memorized so I could let Eli know where I was next time I called him.

"A beach condo? Sweet deal," Alonzo said as he nodded. "Count on seeing me again ... really soon."

Sadie turned from her conversation with Warren and lowered the volume on the stereo. "We can all hook up later."

"Or sooner," Mauve said with a wicked gleam in her eyes.

"You guys better hurry," Sadie interrupted. "The traffic jam is over."

"Hey, Party Girl, be seeing you, too." Warren moved away from Sadie and peered into the back toward me.

"The car behind yours is honking," I told him, pointing.

"We can talk more next time."

Or not, I thought, disliking him strongly although I wasn't sure why.

"Come on, War!" Alonzo called as he turned to leave.

But Warren hesitated, staring at me with that intense look again. "Do we know each other? There's something familiar about you ... Were you at Preston's big bash last month?"

"No!" I said firmly—though I had no idea if it was true.

"Really? You remind me of this girl I saw there. I've got

a great memory for faces...hmmm...guess I'm wrong. Bye, Party Girl." He offered his gloved hand like he wanted to shake good-bye.

But I froze, staring at his glove with its bloody fire dragon design. A horrible suspicion chilled my heart; there was a reason why he'd wear gloves in unseasonably warm weather. What if the gloves were more than a tacky fashion choice? The gloves could be camouflage for glowing gray hands.

Was Warren a Dark Lifer?

Grammy Greta had warned me that Dark Lifers would try to suck my glowing energy by touching me. A brief touch would leave me with a sick, drained feeling like my soul had been violated. I never wanted to go through that. I had to stay away from Warren.

Cars behind us honked as the traffic moved but we remained parked.

"War," Alonzo said. "We have to leave now."

Finally, Warren turned to leave.

But Mauve had other ideas.

"Not so fast," she told Alonzo in a sultry tone. "Aren't you forgetting someone?"

Alonzo couldn't take his gaze off Mauve. "Who?"

With a wicked smile she pointed to herself. "Me."

She clasped Alonzo's hand and before anyone could protest, the two of them raced back to the convertible—and drove off.

Leaving Warren with nothing else to do but go with us.

He took Mauve's place in our car.

An arm's reach from me.

ow do you make small talk with a creepy guy you suspect is a Dark Lifer?

Well, it wasn't easy. At least he was in the front with Sadie,
not back with me. Still, I lied about my seat belt being stuck
and slipped over into the next seat—as far as you could get
from someone inside a moving car.

All the while I was thinking of how I wanted to get
revenge on Mauve. Didn't she care about anyone other than
herself? Even if Warren wasn't a Dark Lifer, being stuck travel-
ing with a random guy was all kinds of uncomfortable. How
could Mauve do this to her friends?

"Mauve is like the best friend ever!" Sadie exclaimed,
her attention focused on driving and Warren. I glimpsed her

dopey lovesick expression when she glanced up at the rear-view mirror.

"Yeah, sweet trade. Two girls to one guy," Warren said. From the back seat, I couldn't see his face but knew he was grinning from his tone.

"I'm just glad to have more time with you," Sadie practically purred. "On a long drive, we can really get to know each other."

"And Party Girl, too." Warren pointed toward me.

"Don't call me that," I snapped.

"Ignore the grouch in the back seat. Rayah has been in a bad mood all morning," Sadie said as if joking, but there was no joking in the glare she shot me through the rearview mirror. "Warren, I think it's amazing you started your own website business. I want to hear all about it."

I tuned out while Sadie ooh and awed over everything Warren told her. A few times Warren tried to bring me into the conversation, but Sadie quickly shifted the topic back to her. It was obvious she wanted all of Warren's attention on her; zero on me.

Did she really think the biggest goal in my immediate life was to steal him? Ha! So far from the truth. I wanted to warn her that Warren might be evil and dead—but she'd never believe me.

I wasn't sure what I believed myself. I could only see the back of his head and one of his gloves, and had no way of telling if he was a dead guy lurking in a stolen body. He acted ordinary enough—except he seemed unusually interested in me. Was he merely curious or waiting for a chance to suck my energy?

"Sadie, can I borrow your cell phone?" I asked, deciding I had to do something or I'd explode from nerves.

"What for?" she asked.

"To call my boyfriend."

"Your boyfriend? Oh, sure!" Her tone was all friendly again. "I didn't realize you were so serious with James."

"Uh…" I gnawed my lower lip, thinking fast. "It surprised me, too."

"Well, I'm thrilled for you. It must be hard going off for a week without him."

"Miserable."

"I can't believe you finally settled on one guy." She flashed me a huge smile. "Maybe I'll get lucky and find someone special, too."

"You never know," Warren told Sadie.

"It's a goal," Sadie said with a significant look at him. "Anyway, Rayah, you can tell James that there's always room for one more at the condo if he wants to join us."

"Sure," I lied.

Sadie reached for her phone, which was propped in a cup holder. But one glance at the phone and she grimaced. "Oh, crap."

"What?" I asked.

"No signal. Too many hills, I guess." She returned the phone to its holder. "You can try later."

How much later? I thought dismally as I glanced out the window. I could see only brown and green hills with occasional oaks or wild scrubs; it was as if we were driving into an infinity of nowhere. A few homes flashed by, but mostly it was empty hills and gravity-defying cows grazing vertically on steep inclines. Traffic continued on sluggishly, slowing then speeding up. We kept to the left, moving swiftly in the fast lane, passing the slow lane where trucks chugged with exhausted effort like out-of-shape joggers. It seemed like we were driving on endless curving ribbons of concrete. Where were the McDonald's, Taco Bells and gas stations?

I shifted uncomfortably, hoping we'd stop soon so I could use a restroom.

When I mentioned this to Sadie, she held up her empty Starbucks cup plus the Diet Pepsi she'd finished. "Me, too," she said with a pinched expression. "These hills are going on forever."

"There's an exit with fast food and gas stations about thirty miles ahead," Warren said. "A pit stop sounds great. It's cramped sitting for a long time." He lifted his arms for a stretch, his gloved fingers reaching out toward me as if by accident. The fiery dragon design seemed to flame like a predator seeking a victim—and I jerked away.

Warren and Sadie kept talking as if nothing unusual had happened, but my stomach rocked with revulsion. Having my energy sucked by a Dark Lifer was personal, and emotionally invasive. But I wasn't positive about Warren, so what could I do? The GEM's advice for dealing with Dark Lifers was to retreat and report.

Unfortunately, in a moving car without the GEM, I couldn't do either.

Fortunately, Sadie kept Warren's focus away from me as she flirted on cruise control. She chattered about favorite foods, music and malls. I'd never been so grateful to be shut out of a conversation. While they talked, I stared out the window, aching to be anywhere else and longing for my real life. What were Mom, Dad, Alyce and Dustin doing right now? Were they back at the hospital, still waiting for me to wake up from the coma? I assumed Sharayah was sleeping in my body, but what if she wasn't? I'd almost been disconnected from life support once already this past week.

How long could I stay away without risking harm to my real body?

It had to be miserable for my family—waiting in a hospital room for me to wake up, unaware I was miles away living someone else's life. I wished I could get a message to them—but even if the GEM rules allowed it, why upset them with the truth? Besides, Grammy had put a lot of trust in me and I didn't want to let her down. If I worked quickly, it would only take a few days to complete my assignment. Then I'd return to myself.

Conversation from the front seat interrupted my thoughts when I realized that Sadie was speaking to me. " … you agree it's nothing like expected?" she asked.

"Um … expect what?" I asked.

"Didn't you hear anything I said?" Sadie glanced back at me with exaggerated drama. "I was telling Warren how we've been planning this trip for weeks and thought we'd already be on the beach by now. It's crazy how nothing is going as planned."

"You can say that again." I sighed, thinking of my friends and family.

"The thing is," Sadie added, "sometimes I get feelings about things that are going to happen, and my intuition says this week is only going to get crazier."

I groaned, hoping her intuition was wrong.

"I'm a fan of all things wild and crazy," Warren said. "I've heard it gets really insane on the beach—lots of music, contests and partying."

"Mauve wants me to enter a wet T-shirt contest," Sadie said. "What do you think?"

"You should." Warren twisted toward the back seat, his gaze narrowing at me. "And so should you."

"No way," I said. "Too embarrassing."

"Rayah, you're such a kidder," Sadie said, giggling. "You're the one who showed Mauve the photos of last year's wet T-shirt contest you found online. And you said you'd be first in line to enter."

"Oh, well...I've changed my mind about entering." I paused. "Standing on a stage and being drenched with water doesn't sound very fun."

"It's plenty of fun for the guys watching from the audience," Warren retorted.

"You would say that," I replied, frowning.

"What's that supposed to mean?" he accused, his muscular shoulders straining at the seat belt as he twisted around toward me. "You know, I'm getting tired of your attitude. I've been really friendly to you, so why are you so cold?"

"He's right, Rayah," Sadie agreed. "You've been rude to him."

"Did I do something to piss you off?" Warren asked.

"Of course not." I squirmed uncomfortably in my seat belt. "I'm just not feeling social after a rough night."

"I warned her not to stay out so late," Sadie added with a

reproachful glance back at me. "Don't take it personal, Warren. She's cool with your being here. Right, Rayah?"

What else could I do but nod?

Time to change tactics, I decided. If Warren wanted to get aggressive, I could, too—but in a more subtle way. Remembering advice from a book on dealing with awkward social situations called *Disarming Your Enemy With a Smile,* I decided to turn this conversation into a fact-finding opportunity.

I summoned my most disarming smile. "If I've been rude—sorry."

"No problem," Warren said.

"Sadie's right, I've been a grouch. I'm a little hung-over still, but that's no reason to take my bad mood out on you."

"I've been hung-over, too, and it bites," Warren replied. "Lucky for you, I give great neck rubs. When we stop, I'll massage away your pain."

And try to suck away my energy, I thought suspiciously.

Trying to be polite, just in case he wasn't an energy vampire, I pasted on a smile. "Sure, that sounds cool." Then, with stealth purpose, I added, "While you're massaging, I'd like to try on your gloves. The dragon design is cool and the leather looks so soft."

"Forget it. No one wears them but me."

"You can't give a massage with gloves," I argued.

"Yeah, I can. It's better that way."

"I'd love a massage," Sadie said, her hand on the steering wheel as she turned toward Warren.

"Sure, babe."

"But Rayah's got a point about the gloves. I'd rather feel your strong hands on my shoulders."

"It's either with gloves or not at all. I don't take them off in public; they're my personal icon." His tone was friendly but when he waved his hands my direction, I felt a chill that made me shiver despite the stuffy warmness inside the car.

Sadie took Warren's words as a challenge and spent the next few miles trying to bribe him to take off his gloves. No matter what Sadie offered, Warren refused. Definitely suspicious.

This would be a great time for another Temp Lifer to pop in. I sent a silent message to Grammy Greta, clasping my fingers together as if praying. And to my surprise, I felt something—a warm sense of calm and a light caress on my shoulder. Then it was gone. Had I imagined it? Or had Grammy given me a pat on the back to encourage me to keep trying?

Only I don't know what to try, I thought, staring down at my hands.

Not my hands. Those pale bony fingers were loaners; without freckles and stubby fingernails. There was a whitish tan line around the ring finger on the left hand that I hadn't noticed before. Sharayah must have worn a ring for months to develop a tan line. I wondered why she stopped wearing it. Did it have anything to do with the mysterious boyfriend Gabe?

As I puzzled over this, a noisy breeze blew in from Sadie's open window, swirling my hair in my face. I inhaled a blend of smog and salty air that made me think of the ocean. We were still far from the Pacific, but I'd be able to see it soon. I loved, loved, *loved* the ocean. I hadn't been to the ocean in a long time, not since my family doubled in size and we were shackled with adorable but demanding triplets. It would be so wonderful to kick off my shoes, run on the warmed sand, and splash in frothy blue-gray waves. I'd have a kick-ass spring break wading in the surf and sunning on the beach. Except, I suddenly remembered, Mauve said Sharayah had an ocean phobia, even had bad dreams about the ocean. How could anyone be afraid of something so beautiful? And how could I pretend to be afraid of something I loved so much?

I am sick of pretending, I thought as I glanced up at Warren's arm stretched across his seat, his gloved fingers a reach away.

"Hey, Rayah! How do you like this station?" Sadie had switched from the CD to the radio, jumping from song to song. She stopped on a familiar song, turning up the volume. "It's that alt blues song you like, 'Bleeding on the Inside.'"

"I love this song," I said, surprised to share musical taste with Sharayah.

"Well, duh, that's why I chose this channel. It's got all our favorite songs. Remember when we sang on karaoke night?" Sadie giggled. "We were so smashed on Long Island Iced teas that you tripped over a cord and knocked us both off the stage. This really cute waiter caught me but you landed on a table. Wasn't it a riot?"

"Oh, yeah," I said vaguely.

"Sing with me, Rayah," Sadie urged. "Let's show Warren how we duet on karaoke nights."

I couldn't! I'd never sung in front of anyone. I had good rhythm, but a voice lethal enough to kill airborne germs.

But the real Sharayah wouldn't refuse.

So I sucked up my shyness and sang along softly with Sadie. She had a nasally voice and a hilarious way of inventing her own lyrics. I didn't know whether she couldn't remember words or she just didn't care. I cringed every time she got a word wrong.

At first I was just playing along, not really thinking about anything, until suddenly it hit me: I didn't suck. Well, Sharayah didn't. I lifted my voice, amazed by its power and absolutely perfect pitch.

"Wow," Warren said when the song ended. "Rayah, you were great."

"What about me?" Sadie pouted.

"Unforgettable," he said.

"I'll take that as a compliment," Sadie said, giving his arm a playful swat. "But I agree that Rayah's a natural. I begged her to try out for American Idol only she refused."

"Talent like yours shouldn't be wasted," Warren told me.

"Don't bother trying to convince her," Sadie said. "Rayah has a great voice but no ambition to do anything about it. Can you believe she's majoring in medicine? Like hanging out around sick people would be more fun than performing in front of millions of fans. She could be a real star if she'd just go for it."

So why didn't Sharayah go for it? I wondered. My "borrowed" voice had full range, passion, and a soulful quality. The hint of dusky vibration added uniqueness—the extra factor the music industry loved. Of course, it took talent to be a doctor or nurse, too, and I had nothing against the medical profession. But a beautiful voice was a gift to be shared with the world, and becoming a star would be more exciting than taking blood pressure. I would give almost anything to have Sharayah's natural talent. Unfortunately, my real voice could scare small children. That's partly why I decided to become an entertainment agent. If I couldn't be a star, I'd create them.

Recently, I'd come close to signing my first client. This new girl at school, Trinidad, wowed me so much with her powerhouse voice that I knew she was destined for stardom. So what if I didn't have any experience as an entertainment agent? How do you get experience without taking risks? Trinidad was so talented that I knew I could convince a studio to sign her (and me!) on. But before I had a chance, the whole body-switch happened.

Now I had a chance to sign up another new talent—myself!

Puzzle pieces flew up in my mind, danced pirouettes, and fell down in perfect place. It all made sense now. This was why I'd been put in Sharayah's body and why we were headed to Venice, not far from Los Angeles where Hollywood dreams come true. It wasn't a cosmic error. I was the perfect person to help Sharayah become a star.

I tingled with the thrill of this "ah ha!" moment, confident I'd complete my assignment quickly. If it meant staying with Sharayah's friends at a luxurious beach condo, well, I was willing to make that sacrifice.

"At last! A gas station." Sadie pointed as she merged onto a right-hand ramp. "And my phone has a signal."

"Great!" I said.

"You can use the restroom first," she told me. "I got some texts to send to my family, but should be done when you get back."

The car came to a stop by the food mart attached to the

gas station. I grabbed Sharayah's purse in case I needed money and scrambled out.

"Wait up, Rayah!" Warren called but I ignored him, picking up my pace.

As I pushed open the glass door, I sniffed the buttery scent of popcorn along with sugary pastries and other yummy snacks. I had plenty of cash—why not spend some of it on food? I drooled a little at a shelf of assorted candy bars, debating on whether I'd rather have a Milky Way, Peanut M&M's or a Kit Kat bar.

I followed a hand-written sign to a restroom far in the back.

The bathroom had a sour odor and only two narrow stalls. One of them was missing a door, so I chose the other.

I was humming to myself, still in awe over the amazing voice coming from my mouth. Lost in starry dreams and all the possibilities, I was only faintly aware of the sound of the door opening. Then the lights went out.

"Hey, who turned off the lights?" I cried.

No one answered, but I heard faint footsteps padding toward the stalls. In the dim light coming from the high windows, two white sneakers seem to glow like eerie ghosts. Instead of heading for the stall adjacent to mine, they stopped outside my locked door.

"Sharayah," said a low voice hissed with hatred. "It's all over."

Through the slit in the door I saw a glint of fiery curls.

The red-haired girl had found me.

And then she kicked the door.

7

A zillion thoughts raced through my head—all urging me to flee. But sitting on a toilet with my jeans bunched around my ankles wasn't exactly a position for a quick getaway. The door was already hanging a little askew from her kick. I didn't think it would survive another.

"Who's there?" I called out, standing and pulling up my jeans.

"You know," she growled.

"No, I don't!"

"Stop lying."

"I'm not!" I cried. "What do you want from me?"

"Come find out," she said ominously.

"I don't want any trouble."

"Too late."

Her tone boiled with fury—and even though I tried not to freak out, I was scared. How could I get away? She blocked the only way out of the room. What if she had a gun or knife? All I had was my purse and its assorted, non-lethal items.

Think, think! I urged myself. In the hundreds of self-help books I'd read, what advice would help protect me from a psycho enemy? My brain blanked. She wouldn't really try to kill me ... would she? I could only see her shoes and a slash of red hair through the gaps around the door. What if she attacked me? Would anyone hear my screams?

"Why did you follow me here?" I tried to sound calm, but my hands shook as I zipped my jeans. "What did I ever do to you?"

"How can you even ask that?" Her voice rose hysterically. "You ruined everything ... but it ends now. Open the door."

Uh huh. No way. Not on my life—literally.

But I couldn't stay in a locked bathroom forever, so what was I going to do?

I was considering crawling underneath into the next stall when I heard sweet sounds—footsteps and the jiggle of the door knob.

Someone was coming into the room!

"Why is it so dark?" I heard Sadie say before she cried, "Hey, what the—!"

There was a slap of sneakers and a gasp.

"Watch where you're going! What's your problem?" Sadie swore as the red-haired girl bumped into her. There was a groan, then the sharp bang of the door slamming. "Rayah? Rayah!" Her voice rose. "Are you in here?"

I nodded, then realized she couldn't see me through the stall door and called out in a shaky whisper, "Y-Yes."

"Why are the lights off? Must have been that bitch." She flipped the light on. "Are you okay?"

"I am now." I sucked in a deep breath, then took a step forward on shaky legs, hooking my purse strap on my arm and unlatching the door.

"What the hell is going on?" Sadie rubbed her shoulder, flipping her braid away from her reddened face. "Did you see that freaking girl who smashed into me?"

"I couldn't see much of anything."

"Damn girl pushed me into the wall and then ran out of here…hey! Why are you hugging me?"

It was impossible to explain right then; my emotions were racing to catch up with my thoughts. I was confused about what had happened and afraid to know what might have happened if Sadie hadn't showed up. Sadie may have just saved my life.

"You're trembling." Sadie studied my face. "What's going on? That girl was familiar, like I've seen her around campus. Do you know her?"

"Not her name—but she's the same redheaded girl who glared at me in the campus parking lot. Thank God you showed up because she sounded crazy, like she was about to get violent."

"No shit!" Sadie did a double-take. "So why are we just standing around? Shouldn't we tell someone?"

"You mean the police?"

"Well…maybe not that drastic." Sadie hesitated, a thoughtful look flitting across her face. "I mean, you weren't attacked, I didn't get a good look at the girl, and you don't even know her name. The police couldn't do anything."

"Yeah," I agreed, thinking how risky being questioned would be when I wouldn't be able to answer routine questions about myself.

"Are you sure you're okay? I've never seen you so scared. Not even when you got that threatening note—" She broke off with a choked cry. "The stalker! Could it be the redhead?"

"I think so," I admitted as I turned on the sink faucet, feeling oddly comforted by the rushing sound of water as I washed my hands. "She must go to our college. Are you positive you didn't recognize her?"

"It was too quick and dark." Sadie ripped off a paper towel and handed it to me.

"Thanks." I wiped my hands. "I won't forget what she looks like and I'll be careful not to let her trap me again. I can't believe she followed us all the way here. I don't even know who she is."

"Well, she obviously knows you. Probably the girlfriend of some guy you hit on—it wouldn't be the first time you pissed off some chick." Sadie giggled. "Like when you were sucking face with Bryanna's fiancé at her engagement party."

"Can we not talk about my past? I'd rather get out of here and far away from that psycho girl. And I could really use your phone."

"I understand." She handed the phone over, then held my arm gently as she led me out of the restroom.

It was surreal how ordinary the gas station's food mart seemed after my short moments of hell. People walked up and down the aisles, absorbed in choosing candy bars and other trivial items. I spotted Warren over by the hot-food area, squirting mustard on a corndog. He arched his brows in curiosity when Sadie called out that we were going to wait by the car.

When I stepped outside, I tensed and looked around for red hair. Logically, I knew the psycho girl wouldn't be dumb enough to wait around. She was probably miles away by now. But if she was obsessed enough to follow me hundreds of miles, she wouldn't give up that easily. She could still be lurking in one of the many parked cars—waiting for another chance to get me alone.

"She's gone," Sadie assured me, guessing my thoughts. She opened the back car door for me. "Talking to James will make you feel better. I'll get us some burgers—no onions, with cheese, right?"

"Uh, fine. Thanks," I told her. Of course I had no intention of calling James.

With the door shut, the outside noises of cars and trucks faded to calming silence. Lifting the phone, I rejoiced to have a signal.

"Eli, it's me," I said as soon as I heard his voice.

"Amber!" Relief, fear, shock merged in this one word.

I found myself smiling despite everything. "It's great to hear my real name."

"Why didn't you call sooner? I've been freaking worried. Where are you?"

"A gas station outside of L.A. I couldn't call until now because we were driving through hills and I couldn't get a signal."

"So what's been happening?"

"Insanity!" I shook my head wearily. "Remember that stalker I told you about? She trapped me in a bathroom."

"You okay?"

"Yeah. Sadie startled her and she ran off. I still have no idea who she is." I sagged against the car seat. "How can I protect myself when I don't know why she hates me?"

"It's not you she hates," Eli said angrily. "I love my sister but she's the one who has enemies. Just get out of there and come home."

"Not until I finish my assignment," I insisted. "Grammy trusted me and I don't want to let her down. I could work faster if I had the GEM."

"I'll get it for you," he promised.

"Is that bi ... Katelyn still helping you?"

"Yeah, Katelyn's been great. She's talking to the resident manager, trying to get a key to Shari's room."

I scowled. "That's so sweet of her."

"She's totally cool," Eli said, totally not getting my sarcasm. "I found out why she hates you ... I mean, Sharayah."

"Let me guess—because of some guy?"

"How'd you know?"

"I'm getting to know your sister ... too well."

"Unfortunately, I know what you mean." His voice ached with misery. "Sharayah has changed so much, in all the wrong ways. When Katelyn was talking about her, it was like she was describing a stranger. Katelyn and Shari got along at first— until Katelyn went out with this guy and he only wanted to talk about my sister. Katelyn was disappointed but thought it was only fair to let Shari know this guy liked her. Only instead of being grateful, my sister flipped out, swearing and shouting at Katelyn."

"Why?" I asked, surprised.

"I have no idea—and neither does Katelyn. They haven't spoken since then."

An idea struck me. "What if the guy was Gabe? We know they were going out, but they must have broken up because Rayah isn't dating him anymore."

"Except the guy Katelyn went out with was named Caleb."

I frowned, confusion mounting as I added *Who is Caleb?* to the mental list of questions I would ask the GEM.

Eli seemed to guess what I was thinking because he reassured me he'd keep trying to get the GEM. "If I can't get someone into the room legally, I'll pick the lock—I think I can do it thanks to tips from your friend Dustin."

"You talked with him? Great! I was going to suggest that before Mauve grabbed the phone out of my hands."

"He asked about you, too, and when I told him you were in my sister's body, he wasn't even surprised."

"You told him?" I said, biting my lip as I thought of the Nine Divine Rules.

"I thought it was okay since you're such good friends."

"Well, it's okay with me—but I'm not so sure about Grammy."

"Your *dead* grandmother?" he asked in a tone that showed he was still getting used to my experiences with the other side.

"Telling anyone about being a Temp Lifer is against rules. I shouldn't have told you," I admitted. "But I'm glad I did. And I'm glad Dustin knows, too."

"He has your back a thousand percent. He was ready to drive all the way here even though we could get arrested for breaking into a girl's dorm."

"It wouldn't be his first arrest. Dust is proud of the hand-cuff scar he got from his first time resisting arrest." My anxiety eased with my laugh. I told Eli how Dustin thrived on political challenges and believed freedom could only come from chaos. "I don't always agree with him," I added fondly, "but I love him like a brother."

"Technically I'm your brother now," Eli said wryly.

"You don't feel like a brother to me."

"Yeah, but hearing your voice, I keep thinking—that's my sister."

"Only on the outside."

"I know ... Still, it'll be weird seeing you."

"Way weird." I paused, wondering what kind of contact was allowed between siblings. Could I hold his hand? Hug him? Give him a "sisterly" kiss on the cheek? Damn, this was going to be so awkward. If talking to him made my hands sweat and my heart pound, what would happen when we were face-to-face?

Before I could discuss any of this, he told me someone was at the door.

"No worry," he said a moment later. "It's only Katelyn."

"Oh, goodie," I said not-so-happily.

"She's grinning like she has good news."

"Oh?" I asked with new interest.

"She's waving a key. Got to go!"

There was a click and the dial tone.

Damn. What was going on with him? Sure, he got the

key and that was good. But not so good was how excited he'd sounded about seeing Katelyn. He hadn't even said good-bye. My emotions were live wires, sparking inside of me and short-circuiting my logical thinking ability. I wasn't jealous. That would be ridiculous. But he was with her, not me, and that made me a little crazy. What I really needed was to talk. Not to just anyone, either, but to my BFF. I'd always told Alyce everything and going for so long without talking to her felt wrong. Like half of me was missing. She already knew that I had a habit of changing bodies, so she wouldn't freak out if I told her what was going on. Sure, it would mean more rule-breaking, but I never kept anything from Alyce.

Only when I called, her mother answered.

"Who is this?" Mrs. Perfetti asked in her typical clipped, irritated tone.

A simple yet impossible question to answer.

"I'm ... um ... Harmony Furrson." This was the name we gave to the pet hamster I'd had when I was seven. "I sit behind Alyce in algebra and need homework advice."

I added the part about algebra because (a) it was true—I did sit behind her in algebra and I hoped Alyce would pick up on that hint, and (b) her mother was militant when it came to homework, even locking Alyce in her room until she finished her assignments.

"Alyce doesn't have homework over spring vacation," her mother said coolly.

"It's extra credit work."

"Then it can wait till school resumes."

"But it can't wait—I really need to talk with her."

"Sorry. Alyce is unavailable." Then she hung up.

What was this? Hang up on Amber day? I wanted to call Alyce back but knew her mother never backed down when she got into one of her moods. So I dialed Dustin's number—which wasn't even breaking GEM rules since Eli had already told him about my body-swap.

When Dustin realized who I was, he whooped like I was Publishers Clearing House calling with a million-dollar offer.

"I was going to visit your body in the hospital but this is much better," he said. "How's everything going?"

"Better since I figured out what I'm supposed to do in this body."

"What?"

"Make Sharayah a singing star."

"Big job! How are you going to accomplish that?"

"By finding an audition or contest that she—I mean, I—can enter, that happens soon and is close to Venice Beach. Can you help?"

"Already on it." I visualized him swiveling in his chair in front of several monitors. He didn't have a bed in his bedroom, preferring a couch with a sleeping bag, conserving his minimal space for maximum strategizing. He called his room his "Headquarters." He was as passionate about his quest for justice as he was with offering help to a friend.

His online search narrowed down the listings to open auditions for amateur singers in the Los Angeles area. He came up with five possibilities, but only two of them would be held soon. One had such a high entrance fee I was sure it was a scam. But the competition for *Voice Choice,* a new cable reality show similar to *American Idol,* was perfect. An open audition would be held in Beverly Hills in two days. Singers had to be amateurs, eighteen to twenty-nine years old with no professional experience—so totally Sharayah.

This was why my grandmother had chosen me for this assignment.

And I wouldn't let her down.

Sure, I had a few obstacles like getting to Beverly Hills, making the finals, wowing the judges and winning the grand-prize singing contract—all while avoiding Dark Lifers and a psycho redhead.

But when I finished, Sharayah would be famous.

And for a brief moment, I would be, too.

A s I handed the phone back to Sadie, it rippled musically with a pop song—and caller ID flashed Mauve's name.

"Where are you?" Sadie demanded.

"Driving," Mauve answered, loud enough that I could hear. "Where are *you*?"

"We made a potty and snack stop." Sadie told her the exit.

"I'll meet you there. Lonz and I aren't that far behind."

"Behind?" Sadie questioned. "I thought you were miles ahead."

"We stopped for lunch and ... well ... let's just say dessert. Details forthcoming." Mauve giggled. "See you soon."

She wasn't exaggerating. In less than five minutes I heard a car honking and saw Mauve's pink hair flying up in the air as Alonzo's convertible screeched into the gas station, burning rubber as it skidded into the parking space beside us.

"Now that's a ride! My next car is so going to be a convertible!" Mauve cried, reaching up for Alonzo's hand as he helped her hop out of the car. "I had no idea my trade idea would turn out so thrilling."

"We've had our share of thrills—but not in a good way," Sadie said ominously.

"Oh?" Mauve asked with a dubious lift of her brow.

Sadie frowned in my direction. "Rayah's stalker showed up."

Mauve's mouth fell open. "I can't believe I missed all the action! I have to know everything." She gave Alonzo a hasty kiss good-bye, explaining that this was "Girls Only" and she'd meet up with him later. When she shooed Warren out of her seat, he looked like he wanted to protest but only shrugged, then climbed back in the convertible beside Alonzo. Within minutes they were roaring out of the parking lot, my tension fading with their disappearing tail lights.

"I can't leave you two alone for a minute!" Mauve complained with a peeved expression as if we'd been having a great time without her. She angled in her seat belt to look at me and demanded to know everything about the stalker.

I really didn't want to talk about that whole freaky encounter—but there was no ignoring Mauve. I couldn't stop wondering, worrying, what might have happened if Sadie hadn't interrupted…

"I cannot believe that bitch followed you all the way here! She's got to be seriously psycho or high," Mauve said, shaking her pink head. "Sure you don't know who she is?"

"I wish I did; then I might know how to stop her."

"I stopped her," Sadie said proudly. "I didn't get a good look at her, but she was scared to get caught. She's long gone by now. She wouldn't have the guts to mess with us again."

I nodded, hoping Sadie was right.

"Too bad I wasn't here," Mauve said as she pulled a lip gloss from a small sequined purse and dabbed at her lips. "I would have smacked her so bad she'd never forget."

"I'll bet you would." I gave a faint smile.

"Hey, you know I got your back after all you've done for me." She paused, her toughness softening for a brief moment, revealing a vulnerability I'd never expected to see on Mauve's face. But then the moment passed, and the don't-mess-with-me attitude returned. "Anyway, the drama is all over—except for what went on with me and Alonzo."

"So what *did* go on?" Sadie asked as she drove out of the parking lot and merged back onto the freeway.

"A lot," Mauve said with a low whistle. "Did you know he's a champion surfer and kick boxer? And those aren't his best talents."

"Oooh! Dish!" Sadie flipped her turn signal and moved into the fast lane. "Anything I can add to the Layaway List?"

"Well..." Mauve drawled. "Let's just say that Alonzo didn't disappoint."

She went on to rave about Alonzo's kissing skills, customized car and tattoos, and about how he was so brilliant he'd been offered an internship in a top law firm. I was skeptical, though, because no guy could be that perfect. Alonzo seemed nice enough, but arrogant, too. The more Mauve described every drama-centric detail, the less I believed even half of it was true.

Still, it was fun to listen.

We were out of the hills now, dipping down into a sprawling metropolis of concrete that stretched on forever with distant towering buildings blending into a gray skyline. Traffic congested; our speed slowed. Sadie didn't seem bothered by the traffic as she kept pumping Mauve for details about Alonzo. Mauve didn't hold much back; some of her answers crossed into the realm of *Too Much Information*. I turned to look out the window, pretending a fascination with LA traffic to hide my reddening cheeks. My body might have been of legal age, but my mind had some catching up to do.

"The ocean!" Sadie shouted suddenly as we left the freeway, pointing to a gap between towering buildings in the far distance. "There it is!"

"I can't see it." I pressed my face against the window, squinting at a horizon of drab, cloudless sky.

"Look beyond those buildings." Mauve pointed.

I'd expected a shade of brilliant blue or green but there was only a gray smudge beyond high-rises. Then I blinked and the gray was gone. Oh well, I'd see the real thing soon enough, I thought with rising excitement.

Mauve pulled out a print-out with directions and told Sadie to keep driving straight for three miles. "Then turn right on Starfish Street and make an immediate left."

"Are you sure?" Sadie glanced over at the print-out in Mauve's hands, frowning.

"That's what the directions say."

"But that can't be right. That would take us away from the beach. My cousin Abigail said the condo had a view of the ocean."

"Haven't you ever been here before?" I asked.

"Don't be stupid. You know I can't stand my cousin. Her side of the family thinks they're better than the rest of us because they're rich." Sadie groaned as she made a right turn. "This can't be the right street."

"Unfortunately it is," Mauve said.

Where are the condos? I wondered, peering out the window at old homes with high porches, rickety steps and fading paint on sagging wood. Junker cars decorated a few dead lawns and I spotted three pit bulls straining at their chains. Yeah, really nice neighborhood—not.

"I am going to kill my cousin," Sadie growled.

"Me, too—after I kill you for trusting her," Mauve added.

"Maybe the neighborhood will get better," I said hopefully.

"It's getting worse!" Mauve griped. "Sadie! Didn't you wonder why the cousin you hate would be so generous to you?"

"I was too thrilled by a rent-free beach condo to ask questions. But I should have known it was too good to be true."

"Look at that dump with all the junk in the driveway. The house is the color of piss and probably smells worse." Mauve complained.

"Um…that dump is our condo," Sadie said miserably as she stopped the car in front of a dilapidated, faded-yellow clapboard home. It had a peaked roof with a tiny attic window that seemed like an evil eye warning us to *leave now*.

"We can't stay here!" Mauve cried.

"I repeat—I'm going to kill my cousin."

Disappointment rushed through me in aching waves. I hadn't realized how much I'd been looking forward to staying by the beach until now. A few hours sunning away my worries in the warm sand would have been wonderful. But we were miles from our beach dreams.

"What do we do now?" Sadie asked, leaning her head against the steering wheel. "It's not like we can afford anything else—assuming we could find anything good."

"Never happen," Mauve agreed. "Even if we had the big bucks for a nice hotel, I've heard they're all booked."

I glanced over at the black purse that I'd tossed on the seat, and thought of the cash inside. This would be a good time to admit I was flush with funds … but suspicions about where the money came from held me back.

"So we have no choice," Mauve decided. She opened her car door and gestured for us to follow. "We go inside."

"Not me," Sadie said with a shudder. "If I enter that dump, I'll have to sanitize my whole body."

"I'm not happy about this either, but it's either go in or go back to the dorm. We have to make this work," Mauve said, gritting her teeth as if preparing to go into battle. "If our rooms are dirty, we'll clean them."

"I'm used to cleaning big messes," I said. "I don't mind hard work."

"You?" Mauve made a *humph* sound. "Your side of our room should be condemned. You can't even find the bed."

Oops. Brain blunder. For a moment I forgot I was supposed to be Sharayah—not the over-worked, underpaid older sister of toddlers.

"Just because I don't take the time to clean," I said defensively, "doesn't mean I don't know how."

"This sucks." Sadie stared out the window with a woeful

expression. "Even if the inside of the house is okay, we can't move it near the beach. Our week is totally ruined."

"It will be with that attitude," Mauve retorted. "We have a place to stay and the ocean isn't that far. Bitch all you want—but I'm going to have fun—damn it!"

I nodded, feeling like I should applaud, but I settled on a small smile.

Sadie grumbled a little more but then followed us up the rickety steps, to a front door where a doormat said: *Home Sweet Hell.* How appropriate, I thought as I ducked under a hanging plant, a green vine poking me in the neck. Rubbing my neck, I waited while Sadie pulled a key out of her pocket and jiggled it in a rusty lock.

"Oh, gross!" Sadie covered her mouth as we stepped into a cluttered living room that smelled like spoiled food and stinky feet.

There were no carpets, only a few stained throw rugs on scuffed wood. Random furniture crowded into the small room: an oval, dark-wood coffee table covered with dirty plates and dishes, a saggy green couch, and four mismatched, worn recliners all facing a large flat-screen TV. Piles of papers filled one corner, a few sad plants wilted on a window shelf, boxes of all sizes were crammed in every empty space, and nearby on the wall, hung crookedly, was a calendar from 1982. Behind a leaning tower of boxes, I spotted a small Christmas tree with several unopened presents—as if time and housekeeping had left this room untouched.

"Still think we can stay here?" Sadie asked sarcastically.

"Well..." Mauve stared around, at a loss for words.

"What's that smell?" I asked, puckering my nose.

"Something died, I think, under those boxes," Sadie said with disgust. "I'm not staying long enough to find out. There's dust on the dust and all that's holding that window together is duct tape. Civilized people cannot live like this."

"Are you sure we have the right house?" I asked.

"Yeah—the key did open the lock. Besides, I recognize that picture." Sadie pointed to a framed photo besides one of the dying plants, of a girl with long dark hair and thick brown glasses. "That's Abigail—before her laser surgery fixed her eyes and she dyed her hair blond. When I see her, I'm going to grab that blond hair and twist—"

We couldn't get out of the "crappo" house fast enough.

Driving to the ocean didn't take long—the real challenge was finding a place to park. We drove in circles until we finally dove into a spot just as a SUV was leaving. Then we made our way down steep wooden steps onto a grainy carpet of sand that stretched across a vast beach to the emerald-blue ocean. It was a clear day, the sea calm and a sweet breeze cooling us.

But the action on the beach was the opposite of calm. Sand stretched as far as I could see, congested like a highway but jam-packed with bodies rather than cars. People littered the beach with blankets, chairs, coolers and shady umbrellas. It wasn't a hot day—the temperature was only in the mid-70s—yet a lot of sunbathers were wearing bikinis. They were stretched out on blankets, playing volleyball and chasing waves. I could taste salty air mingling with the scent of coconut suntan lotion.

"Now this is more like it," Mauve said with a satisfied sigh. Sadie and I nodded in agreement as we looked around the beach.

We hadn't bothered to change our clothes, so we were still wearing T-shirts and jeans. I found a blanket in the car trunk and spread it out on the sand. But I was the only one who sat down. Immediately, I found out we had different definitions of beach fun.

"I spy cute volleyball players," Mauve said with the same wicked light I'd seen in her eyes right before she'd traded herself into Alonzo's car. "Anyone up for some volleyball?"

"Not me," Sadie said. "I want to check out the boutiques."

"Boutiques?" Mauve grimaced at the tacky tourist stores and wild assortment of street performers that lined the narrow road beyond the bike path. "Aren't you ever too tired for shopping?"

"Me? Never!" Sadie said with a laugh.

Both invited me to go with them, but having no idea if the real Sharayah would choose shopping or volleyball, I stayed on the beach. Intoxicated by the peaceful lull of ocean, I just wanted to soak in the sun and surf. Tomorrow I'd figure out a way to get to the *Voice Choice* audition—but for now, this beach was my heaven.

I sank down on the blanket, kicking off my shoes and dangling my toes into the sand: gritty and dry on top, but cool and damp down deeper. Closing my eyes, I luxuriated in the feeling of soft wind and sunshine. The sounds of voices drifted away and I felt myself drifting, too, mesmerized by the steady beat of the ocean's force, the rise and fall of waves lulling me into sleep.

And I dreamed of Gabe.

"We're almost there," said a rugged-looking guy with a long face, a wild tuft of night-black hair, and dark green eyes. He held out his tanned hand to Sharayah. "This step is cracked, so you better hold onto me."

Me-as-Sharayah reached up, smiling, a bursting-with-happiness expression I'd never seen before on her face. But I recognized that look and knew what it meant.

Sharayah was in love.

We were by the ocean, but not the pristine, people-cluttered beaches of southern California. The air was crisper, dangerously darkened by storm clouds and rich with wild winds that swirled up my thick dark hair, whipping its long tendrils against my cheeks. It was strange how even though I was inside Sharayah's body, I was outside, too, watching my fingers curl into the green-eyed guy's strong hands as he helped me up wooden steps that were set into a grassy hill of sand.

And as we crested the hill, a horizon of clumps of wild grass stopped at a sharp cliff overlooking jagged rocks that dropped down into a violent, spitting sea. The bluffs reminded me of the high seats in a movie theater, where you see everything from far away, straddling so close to the edge that it seems you could tumble down into the drama. I knew this guy had to be Gabe—the mysterious passionate love of Sharayah's life. With him, at the top of their world, she was insanely happy.

"When are you going to tell me the surprise?" she asked playfully, breathing a little hard after the climb.

"Isn't this surprise enough?" He gestured beyond the wild green grasses to the churning, gray-green sea that stretched into a curved horizon.

"But I thought...well, you hinted that today was special." And she was thinking how she hoped he had a ring hidden in his pocket, anticipating the many romantic ways he would ask her the Big Question and how she would throw her arms around him, kissing the answer, *yes*.

Of course, her family would be outraged when they found out she was getting engaged to an older guy she'd only known a few months. If they had their way, she'd stay in a protected bubble and never experience anything. But screw them, she thought angrily. So what if they didn't approve? Eli was the worst of all, acting like he was her big brother rather than four years younger. What did he know? What did any of them know? If they gave Gabe a chance, got to know him, they'd love him, too. And she'd show him how much she loved him on their wedding night, taking off the silver *Promise Me* ring she'd worn since she was seventeen, the one she'd put on when she'd made the chastity vow to wait until marriage. Old-fashioned it may seem to others, but to her it was the best way to make sure everything was perfect.

So, for the first time since meeting her soul mate, she tasted the word "yes" on her lips; excited, eager and finally ready to commit; as if everything up until now was a rehearsal for her real life.

They stood atop the bluff, fingers entwined, buffeted by the increasing winds. She pulled her jacket tighter with her free hand, wishing it were summer with blue skies and gentle waves, not the ferocious pounding of a threatening storm. Yet in a way the weather was romantic with its wild intensity, so very unlike all the everyday, neat, planned moments of her LBG.

Life Before Gabe.

"So what's the surprise?" She had to raise her voice to be heard over the wind. In just the short time they'd climbed up, the clouds had rolled in closer, ominously dark, gathering like heavy fists.

"Are you ready?" He breathed his words so close to her mouth they were almost a kiss.

"I've been ready for you my whole life."

"It's been far longer for me," he said with a wry twist to his lips.

Sharayah smiled at him. "There must have been others."

"Only one." He tipped her chin up with his finger. "Only you."

"Exactly as it should be," she teased, trying to sound calm and not like her heart was practically pounding out of her chest. But I could feel her excitement, mingled with fear, and knew the fears she'd worked so hard to hide. She was terrified that she wasn't good enough for Gabe, that she was too young and inexperienced, that he would be disappointed.

He'd confided in her about his travels around the world, the tragedy of losing his family—details he couldn't bring himself to talk about—and how that loneliness drove him out of the country, searching for a place to belong. He'd suffered and experienced so much while she'd lived her whole life in a bubble of the same place, same people, and same daily everythings. She'd had the same best friend since childhood and hadn't even changed the style of her hair, experiencing no more drama than the semester worry of maintaining a 4.0.

Until now.

High on a stormy bluff with the man she loved, she was finally ready to remove her precious silver ring and replace it with another ring, one representing vows to love, honor and cherish forever.

She eyed his pocket. "How long do I have to wait for my surprise?"

"Not much longer."

"Is it a gift?"

"Yes." His green eyes swirled deep with secrets.

"What is it?"

"Are you sure you're ready?"

She nodded.

The wind howled around them and he opened his jacket,

drawing her into his warmth. "Do you trust me?" he whispered.

"How can you even ask?"

"I have to know for sure."

"Of course I trust you. I love you more than I've ever loved anyone. There isn't anything I wouldn't do for you."

"Anything?"

He reached into his pocket and pulled out something round and gray that I thought might be a wrapped box. But when he lifted it up, I saw a roll of duct tape. "Will you show me how much you trust me?"

Sharayah's heart beat faster, wilder, overwhelmed with her feelings for Gabe. She didn't understand this game he was playing, but she was his; mind and soul.

"Yes, Gabe. Anything," she told him again.

"Hold out your hands."

She felt a twinge of uncertainty, but reminded herself that this was her wonderful Gabe. She could trust him with her life. So she held out her hands.

"Thank you, my sweet love," he murmured as he brushed his lips across hers.

Then he brought the tape to his lips, bit off a long strip and wrapped it around her wrists.

"Gabe?" Her voice warbled. "What are you doing?"

"Trust comes without questions."

"But why wrap my hands?" The tape bit tight into her skin, hurting. "Please take it off."

"That's not how this goes." A storm swept across his eyes and the loving softness of his voice tightened like the twine. "Do you still trust me?"

"Gabe, untape me now."

"Do you still trust me?" he demanded.

"I ... I ... yes, I do." She nodded, tears stinging down her windblown cheeks.

"Then you're a fool."

And through blurry eyes she saw him reel back with his hand as if to strike her, so she bent her head forward and butted against him. His feet slipped on the wet grass, the duct tape flew out of his hands and he slipped out of sight, over the cliff.

"Sharayah! Stop screaming! Wake up!"

"Huh?" I jerked up on the blanket, blinking bright sunshine on a crowded beach where voices blended with the gentle rushing ocean waves. Standing before me was Mauve, her pink hair dripping with salty water and sand. The cliffs, the storm and Gabe were gone.

"The ocean dream?" Mauve guessed sympathetically.

I nodded, still shaky. "It was so real."

"It's time you got over your fear of the ocean. Look around at everyone having fun. See, nothing terrible is happening. I won't force you into the water, but you can at least have fun on the beach. Come on!" Mauve urged, tugging on my hand. "I met some of the cutest guys—"

"No!" I stared at her, still swept up in the horror of Gabe. "You can't trust them! They can lie and deceive you."

She gave me a tender look, a towel draped like beach jewelry around her slightly burned shoulders. She'd changed out of her jeans and was wearing a skimpy, neon-blue bikini under a sheer white T-shirt. "Rayah," she said in a softer, compassion-laced tone, "it's just a dream and it's logical you'd have it here. But a dream can't hurt you and doesn't mean anything."

"It has to mean something," I said, feeling off-balance and a little desperate. I found myself looking down at my wrists, remembering the burn of tape but seeing only smooth, somewhat sunburned skin. "What do you know about Gabe?"

"Gabe?" She wrinkled her brow. "Who's that?"

"You're my roommate—don't you know? I must have told you about him."

Mauve's brows spiked curiously as she shook her pink head. "You've talked about lots of guys, but no Gabe. Is he an old boyfriend?"

I hesitated, shivering. "You could say that."

"If he's old news, why do you care?"

"I don't—it's just he was in my dream. Are you sure you haven't met him? Maybe I didn't say his name. He's older, maybe thirty, with a rugged face, thick black hair and green eyes."

"Sounds hot, but not like anyone I know. If he shows up, introduce me … I'd love to meet him."

"I thought you had something going with Alonzo?" I asked curiously.

"Could be. But our vacation only just started so I'm keeping my options open. I mean, just look around." Mauve pointed down the beach to where a huge crowd was gathered. "There's dancing and music, crazy beach games and lots of hot guys. The party won't wait for us—so let's go find it."

She tugged me to my feet and this time I didn't resist, relieved to be led away from nightmares. The brittle edges of the dream images clung to me, leaving me with a sense of fear. Something bad had happened between Sharayah and Gabe. But since Sharayah was alive without any scars, it couldn't have been that dangerous. My subconscious must have jumbled the facts to create that horrible dream. I mean, what kind of monster would tape the hands of a girl after telling her he loved her? What was he planning to do?

That was just sick.

A lingering sense of dread dragged my mood down like a swift undertow. But I tried to shake it off. Here I was—an ordinary high school girl—getting a chance to party like a college girl. Was I going to let a stupid dream ruin everything? No way! When I returned to my real life, I'd have so much to tell Alyce. What I had to share would blow her away.

I took a deep breath of ocean air, then blew out everything negative. This seemed to center me and I felt calmer, the dream fading like fog on a sunny day.

"Rayah! Over there!" Mauve had to shout and lean close to my ear to be heard over the insane noise level. She gestured me to join her as she hurried to join a frenzied group of spring breakers partying by a beach stage.

A DJ ripped out dance music from the stage, and the crowd swayed with hands held high, some of them balancing red plastic cups. I lifted my arms too and sailed on a party wave into a throng of gyrating bodies. It was all so surreal that when some guy in a Speedo offered me a drink, I mouthed the words "thank you" and took the red cup. No one knew (or cared) that underneath this body I was underage. I sipped, puckering at the bitter taste, holding the cup like it was a prop.

As everyone danced, music seeped into my soul and I danced, too. Drinks seemed to magically refill. I sipped away my anxiety, swaying with abandon until all the bad dreams were far from my mind. I couldn't even remember what I'd been stressing about. Something about the ocean—which was ridiculous because I loved the surf, sand, music, partiers, and cute little red cups.

Suddenly it was like—wow! I had lots of new friends! Crowds multiplied, bodies pressed closer together, laughter bubbled like exotic champagne, and I felt fan-freaking-tastic.

"Fun, huh?" Mauve whispered in my ear.

"Oh, yeah!" I raved. "The best time ever."

She nodded, grinning as she clasped my arm, and said something that I couldn't hear. When she tugged on my arm, I guessed she meant for me to come with her.

I kind of floated away as Mauve led me toward a line of girls. I didn't stop to wonder why it was only girls who were lining up, or ask what we were doing here. Thinking too much only caused stress, so I shucked it all off and just gave in to the moment. Dancing, drinking and hanging with my friends. Cool.

"Your name?" A guy with a blue cap squashed down over his sleek black hair sat at a small table and looked up at me.

"Which one?" I giggled.

Mauve pushed me forward and whispered, "Answer him."

"I can't. It's a secret." I giggled. Having two names seemed hilarious, and I was really tempted to tell this nice guy my real name.

"Her name is Sharayah Rockingham," Mauve said, rolling her eyes with annoyance as she spelled out my first name.

"Got it. Here." Blue Cap Guy shoved a plastic card with the number nineteen at me.

The number looked kind of blurry. "What's this for?"

"Stick it on," he told me. Then he looked at Mauve and said, "Next, please."

I turned over the number, trying to decide where to place my number. What was it for, anyway? I'd ask Mauve when she was done talking to Blue Cap. I waited, my skin stinging from the warm sun and my throat dry. I kept sipping my drink—until I looked down and saw that it was empty. I must have spilled it. Oops. Oh well. Someone handed me another one.

Then Mauve bounced over, excitedly waving her number-twenty sticker. "I am so going to score and rock this beach."

I held my number nineteen and squinted at it. It seemed an odd way to sign up to play volleyball but then what did I know about sports? As long as there wasn't running involved, I should do okay. Anyone could hit a ball, right?

"I'm not really good at this," I told Mauve.

"Don't be modest. I've seen you in action before and you're a natural."

"I am?" Hmmm, was Sharayah a jock? Her body seemed too skinny, not toned enough for an athlete.

"Copy everyone else and flaunt your assets."

"Flaunt?" That seemed an odd word to use for volleyball. "What if I fall down?"

"The crowd will go wild and you'll score big."

"You get points by falling? Beach volleyball must really be different than what I played in school."

Mauve stared at me, then sputtered with laughter, spilling the bubbling amber liquid from her red cup to her sneakers. But she didn't seem to notice, she was cracking up so hard. When she came up for air, she gave me a hug.

"You're hilarious, Rayah! If I didn't know how much

you've been looking forward to this, I'd almost believe you didn't know what I was talking about."

"We're not playing volleyball?"

"Yeah, right." She snorted. "You need to take off your bra and change into a tight shirt. Let's go. We're competing in a wet T-shirt contest."

✳

I sobered up fast.

All the way to the car, I tried to talk Mauve out of the contest. If she backed out, then I could cancel too without breaking any GEM rules. But Mauve was determined. She was excited about the prizes, too—eager to win schwag like sunglasses, beach towels or passes to Universal Studios. In my opinion, free stuff wasn't worth being drenched on stage and paraded half naked in public.

Yet this is what Sharayah planned to do, so as her temporary replacement, it was my mission to experience this for her. No matter how humiliating.

"Hurry! Change into something sexy," Mauve told me as she popped the trunk of Sadie's car.

"Sexy?" I stared at her like she was speaking to me in a foreign language.

"Wear your *I'm a Creature of Bad Habits* T-shirt. That should get some laughs and score you some extra votes. Also, ditch the jeans and put on your neon-purple thong."

"A thong! You can't be serious?"

"It'll look like a bikini bottom."

"I'll be practically naked!" I protested.

"If you got it, flaunt and shake it."

"I'm shaking already," I grumbled.

But hey, this was supposed to be fun. Living the college-girl life, finding out what it was like to be older, mature and ... terrified. How was I ever going to find the nerve to get through this? An even bigger question—which one of the suitcases was mine?

Frowning, I studied the trunk crammed tight with a black, a red, and a blue suitcase, plus several bags and a red overnight case. Which one was mine? I was trying to figure out how to ask Mauve when I noticed the initials SR on the black suitcase. One problem solved. Relieved, I clicked it open.

The clothes had been randomly tossed in: shirts, jeans, bras, undies, etc. When I found the purple thong Mauve mentioned, I dangled the micro-tiny suit on one finger and groaned. How was I supposed to fit my ass into this? There wasn't enough material to cover one cheek, much less two.

"Hurry up, Rayah!"

"I'm hurrying already," I snapped.

"Do you hear that cheering, Rayah?" Mauve asked. "The contest is starting without us! You'd better get—"

But I'd stopped listening to her because I'd found something small, round and startling at the bottom on the suitcase. My body went from chilled to burning to numb as I lifted up a tiny silver ring.

I stared at the two-word inscription etched in the band: *Promise Me.*

10

If the ring was real, the dream was real.
And if the dream was real...

Gabe was a monster.

Sharayah had been too trusting. If only she'd listened to Eli's suspicions about Gabe. Then she wouldn't have gone through a horrible betrayal high on that remote ocean cliff. She'd loved him so much, she'd been ready to take off her silver ring and commit to him. So why had Gabe turned violent? Sharayah would have eagerly done anything he asked. It just didn't make sense. She loved him and he seemed to feel the same way about her... until he pulled out the tape.

What was that about? Definitely not love.

I touched my cheek, remembering Gabe reeling back

with his hand as if to strike Sharayah. But instead of hurting her, he'd been the one falling over the cliff. What had happened next? Had he survived? And what about Sharayah? She might not have physical injuries, but there were scars buried inside. Sharayah's heart—the depths of her soul—had been broken. And if Gabe had died, she'd had to live with the guilt of his death. I didn't know the complete horror of what had happened on that cliff, but I was beginning to understand the reason for Sharayah's crisis.

"Rayah!" Mauve smacked her hand impatiently on the side of the car. "Are you ready?"

I jerked around, forgetting where I was until I focused on Mauve's face and the real world rushed back with sounds of voices and surf and traffic. It was jarring to fit the pieces of my memory with all the spring break craziness on the beach. But the silver ring proved I was here for a reason. I slipped it on and made a new promise, both to Sharayah and myself. I would restore her confidence and show her that life could be fun again—even if part of that fun meant competing in a wet T-shirt contest. Heaven help me (and I meant that literally ... Grammy, I could have really used some help!).

By the time I'd changed into the purple thong and the T-shirt Mauve insisted I wear and we reached the stage, number sixteen and her obviously surgically enhanced breasts were shaking up a dripping-wet storm. The crowd—even other girls—hooted for her to take it all off. To my surprise, she did!

"Strategic move. She'll take first place," Mauve grumbled beside me. "I'll have to flash the crowd, too, if I want a chance at winning."

I wrapped my arms around my sheer T-shirt. "Don't even say that."

"What's the harm in a little flash?"

"Aside from the chance it could end up on YouTube?"

"You think?" She actually sounded excited by this possibility. "Now I'm definitely going for it—and you should, too."

"Forget. It."

"Then you'll lose."

"I'm already losing my nerve about going up there."

"That attitude is so not like you. Snap out of it, Rayah."

Oops. I was forgetting who I was supposed to be—not a high schooler with only a few kisses to my name, but an uninhibited college girl. Still, I had a frantic urge to flee, and was coming up with a zillion reasons why this was a bad idea. But then I remembered Gabe's raised hand and the cruel look on his face right before he tumbled off the cliff. Sharayah had gone through so much and deserved some fun. I could do this small thing for her.

But when my number was called, I couldn't make my legs work.

"Go!" Mauve pushed me.

"I-I ... I don't know what to do."

"Dance! Shake your booty! Geez, Rayah, it's not like you haven't danced on a stage before—and wearing much less!"

Mauve gave me another swift shove forward. I found myself front and center on a beach podium beside a smooth-talking DJ who held a mike in one hand and a bucket full of water in the other. I gazed across a sea of heads. All except Mauve were strangers, but united in a mass of shouts and waving hands urging me on.

The being on stage part didn't bother me. I was President of the Halsey High Hospitality Club and had to welcome new students and even give speeches at school assemblies. But this wasn't about speaking or school ... and when a tsunami of icy water splashed over me, I screamed.

"Ahhh! That's cold!"

I stumbled, slipping in puddles and momentarily blinded when my hair dripped in my face. My arms flailed as I tried to keep my balance. My feet slid sideways. To avoid sailing off the podium, I found myself curling into a forward flip—then I landed flat on my feet, like a gymnast. Wow! Where had that come from? Obviously, this body not only liked exercise but knew some cool gymnastic moves.

The audience went wild! I was getting down with the rhythm now, swaying to the music. Pushing my wet hair from my face, I got a thrill from all the waving hands cheering me on. My body seemed to take over again as the music amped up—a jazzy dance song that sent my hips swaying. My skin tingled with goose bumps but I felt warmed from the shouting audience (and probably all those red cups). I danced with abandon, sucked into the rhythm.

What the hell? This wasn't my real life, and the energy sizzling around me was contagious. My inhibitions washed away like the droplets of water streaming down my skin, and I just danced. I hoped when Sharayah returned she'd remember this moment and know that she could overcome anything and dance in her own power.

More shouting, whistling, hooting—a blur of insanity. Then the music stopped and I was ushered off the podium. Mauve slapped me a high five as she hurried past for her turn.

103

A skinny girl covered in tattoos led me to the side of the stage, where I joined the other dripping-wet girls.

Then, amid shouts of "Take it off!" Mauve strutted onto the stage.

When it was all over and the awards were passed out, I was actually disappointed not to place in the top five. Ridiculous to care, right? I never expected to win. I mean, there was little honor or sport in winning because of the "topography" of my temporary body. Still, I'd always had this killer competitive streak and hated losing.

"I danced better than that tattooed girl who took fourth place," I complained while I waited with Mauve to pick up her second-place prize.

"Your flip was cool but I told you about flashing. That's what won me a free sushi dinner for two," Mauve said. "You'll do better next time."

"No next time." I shook my head, which caused me to sway dizzily. "But I'm glad you won and dinner is a cool prize. I could go for some solid food. Unless you've got plans with Alonzo, I'm up for sushi."

"With your allergies?" Mauve stopped to stare at me like I was crazy. "Last time you ate sushi, you swelled up so awful I thought you were dying."

"Well … yeah. I was just joking about eating sushi."

"Rushing you to emergency was *not* funny."

"Sorry," I said, hiding the panic racing through me.

What other important facts didn't I know about this body? Navigating someone else's life was perilous. If Mauve hadn't warned me about the allergy, I might have had an accidental slip. I had to be extra careful or not only would Sha-

rayah miss her chance with the *Voice Choice* competition, but we both could end up dead.

"He's here!" Mauve cried out, bouncing excitedly and waving her hand.

I started to ask who, but knew the answer the moment I turned around and saw the mass of black curls and the megawatt smile. Alonzo had found us. At least I didn't see Warren.

"You made it! I wasn't sure you could find us!" Mauve jumped gleefully into his open arms.

"You're easy to find, babe," Alonzo said huskily, then glanced around. "Where's Sadie?"

"Shopping, as usual. She'll show up eventually." Mauve lifted her coupon and waved it in his face. "Check out my prize!"

"Superior," he said, squinting at it. "Sushi, huh? I'm up for that. So sorry I missed the show."

"Stick around," Mauve said with a suggestive raise of her brows. "I could be persuaded to give an encore performance."

"Keep talking," he urged, pulling her closer.

Awkward third-wheel moment. Wringing out a corner of my dripping shirt, I murmured that I was leaving to change my clothes. We made plans to meet at the car in two hours. Mauve loaned me the car keys and then waved as she hooked her arm in Alonzo's and walked away.

Although my buzz had faded, my head ached and my legs felt rubbery as I left the beach path. How many red cups had I had anyway? At least four ... well, maybe six, but no more than seven. I was following through on Sharayah's plans, but shouldn't I also guide her to better choices? Balancing the role of a Temp Lifer was complicated. Regardless, acting too wild was a bad idea. If I didn't keep a clear head, I'd never succeed at this assignment.

Breathing in and out until my head felt a little clearer, I followed a pathway to the street, dreading another long hike to the car. It had to be at least a mile—maybe even two—and no matter whose body I was in, I detested exercise.

Clouds had rolled in and a breeze shivered my shoulders. I thought longingly of the windbreaker I'd seen in Sharayah's suitcase. What else would I find there? I wondered, pressing the button on a crosswalk. I'd only glanced through it before, too startled by the ring to look any further. This time, I'd take the time for a thorough search without anyone looking over my shoulder.

When the crosswalk light flashed green, I hurried ahead of a large family group pushing strollers. Then I spotted a near-extinct curiosity—a pay phone. Digging into the jacket pocket where I'd shoved some money and a credit card, I trotted over to it and called Eli.

Only he didn't answer.

I left a short "Call ASAP!" message and gave him Sadie's cell number. We hadn't talked for hours, so he should have been by the phone waiting to hear from me. Or was I expecting too much from him? It wasn't like we were officially going out. We'd only known each other a short time—most of it while I was in someone else's body. It was unrealistic to expect him to stop his life for me. But to be honest with myself (a self-help book called *Bullshit Belongs in the Pasture* advised honest self-talk), that's exactly what I had expected. Had Eli grown tired of waiting? This was his spring break, too, so he probably had plans with his family or buddies, plans that didn't include me.

Wallowing in pity, I'd walked a few blocks before I noticed the prickly feeling in the back of my neck. I stopped and rubbed it. I recognized that "being watched" warning. Maybe it was my imagination... or maybe not. Had the red-haired stalker found me again?

Don't turn around, I cautioned myself. Keep walking like nothing is wrong. Force a smile and don't freak out.

I freaked anyway, but only inside my head where no one could see. I could feel the gaze, as sharp as a knife stabbing into my skin. He or she was still close by, and watching.

Although my shirt had dried, goose bumps rippled across my skin. My chill had more to do with fear than the weather, although with the sun dropping the temps had cooled. Nervously, I scanned the street and sidewalk for any sign of red hair. There was a bald guy walking his dog and an elderly couple holding hands while they waited to cross the street. No one suspicious... yet the feeling persisted.

Remembering advice from a book on self-defense, I shifted the car keys in my right hand, knuckling my fingers and positioning the longest key to poke out like a weapon. Of course a key wouldn't protect me from a gun. I had to stay alert and close to other people. I listened anxiously for pursuing footsteps. But traffic whizzed by, making it impossible to hear more than my own thoughts.

So I stopped, bending over in a pretense of tying my shoe, taking a long look around me. But there was no one suspicious.

Puffing out a relieved breath, I straightened and shrugged

off my fears. You're losing it, Amber, I told myself. Imagining monsters and stalkers around every corner is the kind of behavior that results in straightjackets and padded cells. By now the red-haired girl was probably snug in her dorm back in San Jose.

Still, when I spotted Sadie's car, I practically raced toward it. I popped open the trunk and grabbed Sharayah's suitcase. Then I snooped—sifting through shirts, pants, lacy underwear, silky bras, and a low-cut, ruby-red shortie nightgown. There were assorted hygienic items, too, like toothpaste, shampoo, conditioner, breath mints and a box of tampons. Nothing interesting—although I was pleased to find the navy blue windbreaker, which I immediately put on. Then I grabbed a pair of gray sweatpants, which I slipped over the tiny purple thong. There were pockets, and since I'd been uncomfortable carrying so much money in a purse, I shoved Sharayah's wallet in the deep pocket of the sweat pants and hid the purse (with all that cash) in the suitcase.

I had just slammed the suitcase shut when I heard the unmistakable sound of a footstep behind me. Before I could turn around, a hand clamped down on my shoulder.

A gloved hand.

11

"Been looking for you, Party Girl," Warren said with a sly smile and a drunken slur in his voice.

Whirling around, I jumped back and stared nervously at his gloves, imagining gray fingers underneath the leather. I backed away, holding out the point of the car key.

"Don't call me that." I tried to sound tough, but my voice came out like a squeak.

"Hey, I'm just being friendly." He towered over me like a brawny mountain, and even though Sharayah was a tall girl, I felt as small and defenseless as a mouse.

"I'm kind of busy right now," I added with a gesture to the open trunk.

"Too busy to hear your friend's message?"

"Which friend?" I asked warily.

"The one with weird hair."

"You mean Mauve?" I asked.

"Yeah." He nodded. "She asked me to find and bring you to her."

"Thanks, but you can tell her I'll wait here for her like we planned."

"Plans change." He leaned forward against the car, smiling in a way that gave me chills. "Relationships change, too. Like even if there is some other guy, I can't ignore this vibe growing between us."

"What vibe?" I asked, a little scared. "I told you I have a boyfriend."

"Lucky guy. You're looking really fine."

"I'm a soggy mess," I said as pushed back my wet hair and zipped up the windbreaker.

"I like your natural look."

But I didn't like the unnatural look he was giving me—like he could see right through my windbreaker. Or was he something more? When he stared at me, was he seeing an otherworldly glow that was invisible to normal humans? Take off your gloves, I wanted to say. If I could see his hands, I'd know if he was a Dark Lifer. Since suspicions weren't proof, I had to find out for sure before I tried to alert the Dark Disposal Team.

The street that seemed chaotic a moment ago was now eerily quiet—empty crosswalks with no pedestrians, and only a few passing cars.

"Come on," he said, reaching out for me.

I jumped back and shook my head. "I'd rather wait here."

"But Pink Hair specifically asked me to bring you."

"Tell Mauve I have other things to do," I told him hastily. "I'll catch up with her later."

"And miss the party?" He folded his arms across his chest, frowning at me.

"What party?"

"What'd ya think I'm here for? Mauve asked me to bring you too. Don't make them wait, okay? Come on."

"Is Sadie there, too?"

"Who?" He scrunched his forehead as if he'd forgotten flirting with Sadie. "Oh, yeah," he said with a nod. "She's there, too."

I leaned against the car, reluctant to go anywhere with him. "I thought Mauve and Alonzo were headed for a sushi restaurant."

"No one told me about that, but I guess they changed their minds. Ask them yourself." His shrug drew my gaze to his beefy shoulders and muscular arms. Underneath his gloves I knew his hands would be strong, too. "It's gonna be one hell of a party. You don't want to miss out."

Actually, I did, but Sharayah wouldn't refuse so I couldn't either. I nodded reluctantly as I slammed the trunk.

When he reached for my hand, I pretended not to notice and turned away. I held tight to the car keys, the sharpest key still between my fingers, as I walked away from the car, resting my hand and the keys in my jacket pocket. I felt his gaze keenly on me. I resented his attitude toward Sadie—acting like he didn't even remember being with her in the car for over an hour. Dark Lifer or not, he creeped me out and I wasn't going to get near him.

I expected him to go to the crowded beach where I'd sunned earlier, but he veered away from the ocean onto a paved walking path.

"Isn't the party at the beach?" I asked.

"No, even better. It's in a private room."

The path curved, leading away from the hustle and the voices drifting on beach breezes toward an area of small buildings. As afternoon dimmed to early evening, the burnished-gold sun sunk below the horizon and the wind whipped stronger, swirling sand and bits of trash across the path. In an opening between buildings, I could see distant fierce waves crashing against the beach. In a short time, we'd traveled very far away from spring break action.

"Where exactly are we going?" I asked uneasily.

"I told you—a party."

"But there's nothing out this way." I gestured to the blocky warehouse buildings surrounding us.

"The best parties take place behind closed doors after the sun goes down. We'll have music, piles of food and booze. It's just past that tall building."

"I don't hear any voices. You sure this is the right way?" I asked, frowning.

"Party central here we are," he said as we reached a squat building called *Pedal Power*. It was crowded with bicycles built for one and for two, and canvas-covered surreys for larger groups. The sign on the door read *closed*.

"A bike rental shop?" I questioned.

"There's more room inside than it looks from the outside," he assured me as he moved toward the door.

"I don't hear any music." I hung back, reluctant to go in.

"You will once we get inside." He reached into his pocket and pulled out some keys. Stepping toward the door, he flt a key into a lock and jiggled. The door opened with a creak. "Follow me."

Instinct said to turn around and run the other direction. But what kind of adventurous attitude was that? Definitely not how wild Sharayah would behave. And I was here to have fun, right? Not act sensible and boring. Besides, I was in a strange city with only Mauve and Sadie for support, and getting separated from them could be disastrous. Given my infamously bad sense of direction, if I tried to find my way back to the crappo condo solo, I'd probably end up in another state.

So even though the sensible Amber voice in my head screamed in protest, I followed Warren. We entered a dark, cave-like room with a rough cement floor and dank musty odor.

"Where is everyone?" I bit my lower lip.

"In the back."

"This building didn't look that big." I was getting a bad feeling. "Weird place for a party."

"Depends on the kind of party."

"What do you mean?" I asked as he closed the door, shutting out sound and light. "Why is it so dark?"

He didn't answer. I heard the shuffle of his feet, then the click of a light switch. The room burst with yellowy light from a hanging bulb. Score a point for my intuition, but subtract a hundred points for my stupidity. There was no party, no one else—only a dank warehouse with bikes stacked against the walls.

"Warren, you're an ass!" I wheeled on him, spitting fury. "I am so out of here."

I moved toward the door but he moved quicker, sidestepping to block my way like a muscular wall.

"Don't rush off," he said in this lazy, amused tone like he thought we were more than friends. "We can have our own private party here without any interruptions."

"I do not want to party with you. I cannot believe you pulled this! Are you insane?"

"Come on, babe, play nice." Grabbing my arm, he yanked me toward his chest. "I've been talking to some buddies and heard a lot about you."

"You don't know anything about me—and you're a liar! Mauve and Alonzo never planned to come here."

"So what? We're here and that's all that matters. I knew you just needed to get away from everyone so we could get to know each other better. I know what you really want."

"What I want is to get the hell away from you!" I choked out as I tried to shake off his grip. But his arms were steel and his grip like handcuffs.

"Don't be that way."

"I'll be whatever way it takes to get the hell away from you!" I was so angry I couldn't think straight. With a fierce yank, I broke free of his grip, kicking hard and striking his knee.

"Ouch!" He grabbed his knee, jumping in pain. "Why'd you go and do that?"

"I meant to kick higher."

"You little bi—" he swore as he lunged for me. I scrambled toward the door, but before I could grab the knob he grabbed me, his grip much rougher. "You're not going any-where until we have some fun."

"Back off," I cried, wincing as his gloved fingers squeezed my arm. More than ever I was sure he was a Dark Lifer, and I had to get out of here before he took off his gloves.

"You know you like this."

"No way! Even if I was interested in you—which I'm totally not—I already have a boyfriend."

"He's not here." He pulled me closer and I kicked and squirmed. "I am."

"Get away from me!" I screamed.

"You're starting to piss me off." He grabbed a handful of my hair, jerking hard so my face was close to his. "I'm not asking for anything you haven't done before," he added in a softer, cajoling voice. "You wouldn't want me to think you're being a tease, would you?"

"I don't care what you think. If you don't open that door immediately, I'm going to press charges."

"Then I better make this worth the trouble. Come on, baby." He chuckled, his breath smelling like hot beer. "I knew you were into me when we first met. I could tell from the way you kept staring at me. But you didn't want to upset your girlfriend, which I can respect. Sadie is okay, but she talks too much. I prefer the quiet, spunky type—like you."

"Well, I don't prefer you. Back off!" I aimed a kick that would have scored right where he'd hurt the most, but he blocked me.

"So you like to play rough? Me too."

"You think this is playing? Can't you see I am totally not

into you? I don't care what you've heard, I'm not like that and I have no intention of doing anything with you."

"Don't be such a tease." He pressed his face close to mine and I struggled, but couldn't get out of his grip.

Grammy, I thought frantically. *Where are you when I need you? I can't handle this on my own. Please send help!*

But there was no whisper from the other side, only the disgusting breath of Warren pressing his face close to mine. I turned my head, squirming, kicking and screaming. I flashed back to my dream of Gabe attacking Sharayah by the ocean. I wasn't far from the ocean now, and although not on the edge of a cliff, I was trapped with someone dangerous. Instead of a memory, had that dream been a warning? I should have known better than to go anywhere with Warren.

His gloves dug into my flesh, burning, the red dragon design blurring through my tears. What would happen when he took off his gloves? I didn't have a chance against Warren's brute strength. He'd suck my energy and soul until there was nothing left.

"No!" I sobbed as his lips crushed down on my own. Squirming, I grabbed the keys in my pocket and lashed out at him.

"Bitch!" He twisted my arm painfully as he reached up to touch his now-bleeding cheek. "That wasn't part of the deal. Try that again and I really will hurt you."

He came at me once more and I screamed as shrill and loud as I could. But he didn't back off, pressing his face against mine, his lips crushing, stealing my breath so I couldn't breathe. I was suffocating, alive. My head floated, pain and fear making me dizzy. Still, I kept kicking, struggling—

Then the door crashed open and someone shouted, "Let her go!"

"This is a private party—get the hell out!" Warren's cruel grip dug into my wrists.

"I said to let her go." The voice was deep, masculine with a hint of an English lilt.

Torn between fear and relief, I continued to cling to the keys clutched in my hand.

"I'm so scared." Warren snorted like it was a big joke.

"You should be" was the reply.

"You want to take me on?" Warren laughed darkly. "I'd like to see you try."

"No." The English lilt dropped to a growl. "I guarantee you—you would *not* like it."

Then my rescuer stepped forward into the artificial yellow light of the cavernous room: a tanned young man with full lips, thick black brows, and a blue cap with an anchor emblem over a mid-length, dark-blond ponytail. He wasn't exactly handsome, but he had an indefinable charisma. He moved slowly, a sea of calmness despite the turbulence ahead.

Warren shifted, his grip on me loosening, and I took my chance and flung myself away from him with so much force that I stumbled against the wheel of a surrey. Something sharp poked my leg and I cried out with pain. Tears filled my eyes as I collapsed on the hard concrete.

"Who the hell are you?" Warren demanded.

"Someone who's going to smash your face if you don't stop abusing your girlfriend."

"I'm not his anything!" I yelled out.

"I rather guessed that." The stranger's pale eyes narrowed with a focused intensity.

"Screw you," Warren snapped. "Butt out—this doesn't concern you."

"It does now." The words were spoken lightly, but the stranger's gaze was serious.

Warren snorted. "You're an idiot if you think you can take me. I got at least fifty pounds on you and more muscles than you'll ever have."

"That you do. But muscles aren't everything."

"Yeah, right. Like I'm scared. What can a skinny dude like you do to me?"

"This," the stranger said in a low, menacing tone.

Then he whipped out a knife, snapping open a blade that flashed blood-red in the dim light, and lunged to stab Warren.

12

I screamed, scrambling away, suddenly more afraid of the stranger than Warren.

"You're crazy, man!" Warren moved quickly, dodging the sharp knife. "You could have killed me."

"I still might."

"What's your problem? I didn't do nothing to you."

The stranger rubbed the dark-gold stubble on his chin with the blunt end of his knife, seeming to consider the question before answering. "I can't stand idiots who speak in double negatives—and hurt girls."

"Double what?" Warren backed into a stack of bikes. "And I didn't hurt her."

"Not from my prospective," he said as he thrust his knife out again, advancing on Warren.

"Hey, cut it out! I don't mean cut—I mean, lay off!" Warren sputtered, his bravado swept away in the whoosh of a blade. "Can't we talk this over? I wasn't hurting anyone. Rayah and I were just having fun."

"You have a warped definition of fun. I have my own definition—would you like to see how fun this feels?" The knife flashed, whipping past Warren's arm.

"Okay, okay!" Warren scrambled out of the way. "Put that down and I'll do whatever you say."

"You will?"

"Yeah, yeah, just cool it. I won't mess with Rayah again."

"I don't believe you," the stranger said, his knife hand still sweeping toward Warren. "Convince me."

"How am I supposed to do that? I give my word I'm telling the truth! I don't want trouble." Warren lifted his hands in surrender, brushing against the wheel of an upside-down bike and setting it spinning. "Put away the knife! You're sick, dude!"

Before the stranger could come after him again, Warren swore and bolted for the door, fiercely yanking it open and then running away with surprising speed, a shadowy blur disappearing into the twilight.

And I was alone with the knife-wielding stranger.

Um … should I thank my rescuer or run out of the room, too?

Huddling in my jacket, heart racing, I stared up at him, scared yet intrigued. He folded the blade of the knife and tucked it into a pocket. The wind from the half-open door whipped his unbuttoned denim jacket around his lean body. His skin glowed with the deep, bronzed tan of someone who spends long hours outside. A surfer, I guessed, as I admired how his sun-drenched skin complemented his hazel eyes and the chestnut waves in his sandy-blond hair. His hands were calloused and strong, like he spent a lot of time doing physical labor.

Glancing down at the floor, I noticed his navy blue cap. I picked it up and held it out to him. "Is this yours?"

"Right. I didn't realize it had fallen off," he said as he reached out, not actually touching me but brushing so close that the hairs on my skin seemed electric. "This cap has traveled a long way with me—it was a gift from the captain of the first ship I ever sailed. I would hate to lose it. Thanks for noticing."

"I'm the one who's grateful," I said. "What you just did ... um ... I hardly know how to thank you enough."

"You don't need to. Like Cicero says—" He paused with a distant look, and then quoted: "*Gratitude is not only the greatest of virtues, but the parent of all others.*"

Literary quotes? From a guy who looked like a surfer but used his knife like an action hero? Now I really didn't know what to say. I didn't know anything about him. Not even his name.

As if reading my mind, he smiled. "By the way, I'm Dyce."

"I'm Amb ... Sharayah. My friends call me Rayah and you can call me that, if you want, or whatever you like."

"I prefer Sharayah ... sounds like the sigh of a soft sea wind. *As winds come lightly whispering from the West, Kissing, not ruffling, the blue deep's serene.*"

"That's beautiful. Poetry?" I guessed.

"Right. Lord Byron."

"Cool. The only poems I know are silly ones my grandmother taught me when I was little. How can you remember so much? You must have an amazing memory."

"Not so amazing." He fit the cap on his head at a crooked angle, so the anchor design tilted over his right ear. "I just read a lot of old books."

"I do, too. Well, except not old ones, usually self-help books. Unfortunately there wasn't one about how not to be tricked into going into a deserted warehouse with a lying jerk." I glanced around at the shadowy bicycles and shuddered. "This place is creepy. Let's get out of here."

I started for the door but Dyce moved faster. "After you," he said politely as he held open the door—in a gesture right out of one of those old books he liked to read.

When the door shut behind us, it was a relief to inhale the cool, salty evening air. I was feeling other emotions, too, but I was afraid to analyze them.

"Sorry about roughing up your friend," Dyce told me, the gold strands in his hair shining under an overhead light as he leaned against the side of the building. "I can't stand guys who push girls around. But just so you know, I had no intention of cutting him—only scaring him."

"You succeeded. Warren looked scared enough to pee his pants."

Dyce laughed—a low, sexy laugh that made my heart jump. Sexy, smart and chivalrous. Wow, what a combo. Most guys wouldn't even know what chivalrous meant—but Dyce could probably spell it *and* use it in a poem. And let's not forget the fact that he was Class A super-fine. I couldn't resist some inner tingling at his charm, intelligence and the whole rescuing-me thing.

"Just so you know, Warren is no friend of mine," I added, not wanting him to think I was chronically stupid.

"I guessed that," he said.

"I only just met him today, when my roommate hooked up with his friend. I wouldn't have come here with him if he hadn't lied to me about meeting my roommate at a party. But no party and no roommate. I was stupid to believe him."

"You never really know anyone."

"That's for sure," I murmured with a glance down at myself.

"Be careful who you trust and you'll do fine."

"But I didn't trust Warren—he made me suspicious right off. He had this rude way of staring at me. But I tried to ignore it because we were stuck together for a long drive and my friends liked him—especially Sadie."

"Your roommate?" he guessed.

"No, that would be Mauve. Sadie—she's the talkative one—was really into Warren and I thought he was into her, too, until this." I gestured toward the bike rental building. "But why would he go to all the trouble to get me here when Sadie wanted him?"

"I can think of several reasons," Dyce said, a soft cadence to his voice that would have sounded cheesy coming from anyone else, but sounded classy coming from him.

Dangerous conversation territory ahead, I told myself. So instead of asking the most obvious question, I shook my head firmly. "If you met Sadie you'd know what I mean. She's really sweet. Warren was an idiot not to hook up with her and to go after me—especially when I made it clear I couldn't stand him."

"Maybe he's looking for a challenge," Dyce suggested.

"I think it was more than that … something personal. But you showed up before he could … well, anything."

A cool ocean breeze snaked inside my jacket and I wrapped my arms around myself. I peered around uneasily, as if Warren could be lurking behind shadowy bushes, waiting to jump out and grab me. Everything about his behavior had been suspicious, and I was more positive than ever that his dragon gloves had nothing to do with fashion and everything to do with hiding a telltale glow.

I imagined Warren taking off his gloves and pressing glowing fingers into my skin. Realizing what almost happened made me nauseous. Or maybe it was the combination of lack of sleep, missed meals and too many sips from red cups. I didn't realize I was swaying until Dyce moved to my side, slipping his arm around my waist to steady me.

"Sharayah, take some deep breaths," he said gently.

I did as told. His callused touch sent warm waves through me and I started to feel better—for all the wrong reasons.

"I'm okay," I assured as I stepped away to show him I wasn't a pathetic wimp. "I don't usually get dizzy."

"Shock will do that—sneak up like a sleeper wave then knock you over before you know what happened."

"Well … I'm fine now. Today has just been totally insane."

"I understand," he said, nodding. But of course he didn't— and I couldn't explain.

"Getting away for spring break was supposed to be fun," I added, "but nothing has turned out like I expected."

"Not all bad, I hope?" he asked with a lift of his brows.

"Not all," I admitted in a silky tone that would have made the real Sharayah proud but left me embarrassed. Would he think I meant he was the only good thing about today? That I was hitting on him?

"What I meant," I quickly amended, "was that I had a good time on the drive down here with my friends."

Saying this aloud made me realize it was true. The drive had been fun. Not the part where I was cooped up in the car for umpteen-zillion miles. What I'd enjoyed was being accepted as an equal by older girls and experiencing the wild side of college, with complete freedom to do or say whatever I wanted. Also, there had been a sense of girl-connectivity with Mauve and Sadie, sharing stories, sick jokes and gossip. And I could even admit (exclusively to myself) that strutting on a stage wearing only a wet T-shirt and thong hadn't been *that* horrible. Embarrassing? Yes. Terrifying? Definitely. But the flip side of terror is excitement, and being in a borrowed body had given me the freedom to lose my inhibitions, to let loose with wild spontaneity. I could still hear the roar of cheers and applause from the crowd.

I realized Dyce was staring at me. "Anyway, I'm fine now, although things could have gotten critical if you hadn't showed up." I was babbling like I always did when nervous. "Not many guys would bother helping someone they don't even know. Thanks for the rescue and for not actually killing Warren."

"He got lucky." Dyce arched his brows wickedly.

He wasn't the only one, I secretly thought, feeling as if

Sharayah was momentarily in control as she tilted my head and smiled in a slow, seductive way. The logical part of me (let's call her Amber) struggled to gain control, but exhaustion made it hard to focus. I wasn't sure what I was thinking anymore. This body was responding to Dyce—pulse racing, head light, heat surging as if my skin were on fire. Amber warned: Walk away from the hot guy. But reckless Sharayah ignored her.

Dyce wasn't helping things either, staring at me with an intensity that went beyond casual flirting. So I did what any normal girl with normal desires would do when stuck in the hormone-raging body of adventurous spring breaker.

I studied him right back.

His thick lashes were unusually long and curly for a guy, drawing me in into his gray-green eyes, sea-deep with flickers of sun shining across the surface. I found myself wondering what he was thinking. Was he attracted to Sharayah? Not me, of course. He had no idea a high schooler lurked beneath this mature body. My inner Amber screamed for me to walk away before I was swept up into a storm of trouble.

But trouble sounded kind of fun.

"Do you live around here?" I asked him.

"No." He shook his head. "Just on vacation."

"Spring break?"

"You could call it that, although I don't get into all the partying."

I started to say "Me too," until I realized that would be Amber speaking and out of character for Sharayah.

"Too bad," I said, flashing what I hoped was a sexy smile. "My friends and I came here to have a good time, so we'll be doing lots of partying."

126

"It didn't look like you were having a good time when I first saw you."

"I was an idiot for believing Warren. Thank God you got rid of him—but how did you know? Are you psychic?"

"Nope. I heard you scream while I was out collecting driftwood. So I dropped my wood and ran right over."

"You lost your driftwood?" I asked.

"No sweat. I can always find more. I hadn't gathered any decent pieces anyway."

I considered asking why he collected driftwood but that somehow seemed too personal—and my libido was already dancing with danger being so close to him. *Down, girl,* I thought to Sharayah. Flirting was harmless, but nothing else was allowed. Eli was the one and only guy for me.

The problem was ... Eli wasn't here.

Dyce was.

My skin tingled as my thoughts raced in the wrong direction. I'm always going the wrong way at the worst times, I thought nervously. I stared down at my hands, clutching them together so I wouldn't give in to my (very bad!) desire to reach out and touch Dyce. I'd never met anyone like him. Danger and mystery swirled around him, as subtle and seductive as a sea breeze. Deep inside me something wanton and wild rattled the cage bars, eager to break free.

"I have to leave now," I said firmly, more to myself than Dyce.

"Can I walk you somewhere? It's getting dark."

"There are plenty of lights, so I can find my way." Far away from temptation, I thought.

"Still, I don't feel right letting you go off alone."

"Warren wouldn't dare come back—you scared him so bad he's probably left town. I'll be fine. I don't want to keep you from your, um, driftwood any longer. I have to go find Mauve and Sadie. They're probably waiting back at the car and wondering where I am—especially since I still have the car keys." I held out the key ring.

"Go on then." His smile, right into my eyes, increased my reluctance to let him go. He'd been so kind to me—a real hero. He said "good-bye" and started to turn.

"Wait!" My heart pounded as I stepped toward him.

"What is it, Sharayah?" The way he spoke her name rippled like music through my ears and into my heart.

"After everything you've done, I should do something for you—a reward, or maybe buy you dinner," I babbled. "I mean, you may have saved my life."

"You don't owe me anything."

"But I want to thank you. At least let me buy you a drink."

"As much as I'd love to accept, I can't. I need to return to Emmy," Dyce said with a tip of his cap.

"Oh ... I understand."

Emmy. Of course Dyce had a girlfriend—a great guy like him wouldn't be single. And it wasn't like I was without commitments, either.

I reached out to wave good-bye but Dyce misunderstood, clasping my hand to shake it. When our fingers met, I held on—his firm touch was stirring up my willful emotions, dousing the fire of logical Amber. The way he met my eyes, his gaze compelling and his faint dimples enhancing his smile, hinted at mysteries of "what could be" between us.

Not that I was flirting with him or anything.

I was just being polite and showing my gratitude, like anyone would do after being rescued. This had nothing to do with passion, desire, longing…

Get a grip! I ordered myself. Dyce was too old for me— even if I didn't already have Eli. And it would be unfair to risk Sharayah's heart on some guy who already had a girlfriend. She wasn't here to make important decisions, so it was up to me to protect both of us.

Besides, Dyce was going back to his Emmy.

And I had a temporary life to resume.

Still, I couldn't help but wonder… would I ever see him again?

My thoughts were all about Dyce as I retraced my steps down the path, replaying what he'd said and what I'd said back—which now seemed so lame that I burned with shame. What had I been thinking? Drooling at him and practically begging him to let me buy him a drink. Did mature college girls say stuff like that? I didn't think so.

Good thing I'd probably never see him again.

As I reached a shopping area bordering the beach, I recognized Sadie's dark braids. She was moving briskly despite carrying bulging shopping bags.

"Sadie!" I called but my voice carried away in a salty breeze and she didn't even glance my way as she entered an artsy boutique.

So I hurried after her.

The store, called *Life's a Beach*, displayed summery hats, T-shirts, swimsuits and colorful beach towels. Wind chimes jangled as I stepped in, squeezing past shelves crammed with cheesy beach souvenirs, from personalized key chains to glow-in-the-dark flip-flops. The narrow aisles were congested like rush-hour highways, so it was slow going while I searched for Sadie. Finally I spotted her—behind an inflated giant beach ball, weighed down with three enormous shopping bags.

Moving toward her, I started to call her name—then stopped with my mouth frozen open. Sadie had been adjusting the straps on her bag with one hand, but her other hand had snaked out toward a rhinestone watch. There had been a quick flash of fingers, like a magician's disappearing act. Now you see the watch—now you don't.

Before I could decide how to react, or even what to think, Sadie caught my reflection in a mirror on a glass counter.

"Rayah!" She whirled around to face me, scowling. "Where have you been? It's about time you showed up."

"Time … um … " I glanced at the tray of sparkling rhinestone watches in their rainbow reds and purples; they were pretty but made of tacky plastic and priced under ten dollars. How time flies—especially with Sadie's quick-fingered help.

But was I sure what I'd witnessed? Why would Sadie bother to steal? She wore ultra-chic clothes, kept her hair and nails manicured and smelled of costly perfume. She had no reason to steal a cheap watch.

"I hope you have a good explanation," Sadie accused me, her ruby-glossed lips pursed angrily.

"Me? But you just—"

"Where have you been?" She didn't wait for me to answer. "I've been back to the car twice, walked the beach at least a hundred times and even checked the restrooms, which were seriously gross. I've been looking all over!"

"You have?" I shook my head, confusion making my head ache. Nearby, a clerk with pierced eyebrows narrowed her black eyes and watched me closely, as if my overall wind-blown, anxious attitude set off her suspicions. Ha! She had the wrong girl. But I couldn't rat out Sadie.

Sadie's shopping bags swayed, her hands waving as she talked excitedly. "Mauve said we'd meet back at the car but no one was there. I planned to leave my bags there, then go out to eat. But I couldn't find anyone and carrying all these bags was killing my arms. So I called Mauve and she said she was still with Alonzo and would hook up with us later. She told me you had the keys to the car and that you'd be waiting there. Only you weren't."

"Sorry, but I've had some … um … problems." I hesitated.

How much should I tell her? She'd been clear about her feelings for Warren and would be hurt. Worse—she might not believe me. And there was the whole shoplifting thing, too. Both topics I didn't have the energy to discuss in the middle of the crowded store.

"Where exactly is Mauve?" I asked.

"Some sushi restaurant." Sadie waved her hand, a turquoise and gold ring I'd never seen before sparkling from her pinky finger. Was it shoplifted, too?

"Oh, so she did go there," I said with a nod. "I thought she and Alonzo changed their plans."

"You thought wrong. Who told you that?"

"Um...I don't remember." Inside, I seethed—more lies from Warren the scumbag. "Anyway, I'm really sorry you couldn't get into the car. But I'm here now, so let's go put your stuff away...unless you're not finished shopping."

"There's nothing for me in this tourist trap."

"Sure there isn't something you want to buy?" Or pay for, I thought.

"No. I'm done shopping—for today anyway," she added with a laugh. She patted my arm and gave me a little push. "Come on, let's get out of here."

Reluctantly, I followed her out the door, the sound of wind chimes echoing in my head.

"Mauve wants us to join her later at a dance club called Revolution," Sadie told me as we walked to the street. I was now carrying two of her bags.

"I don't have enough energy for standing. Dancing? I don't think so." A truck whizzed by us, stinking of exhaust and whooshing up a breeze that tangled my hair.

"Have you eaten dinner yet?" Sadie asked.

"Dinner? I can't even remember lunch."

"This is not the time to diet. You're already too skinny, anyway. Let's pick up something to eat."

But as we neared the car, it was guilt that was gnawing at me more than hunger. In the store, I hadn't tried to stop her. Did that make me an accomplice? It wasn't too late to do the right thing. All I had to do was tell her I knew she stole the watch and that she had to return it. But I didn't know her that well and was afraid of how she'd react. What would the real Sharayah do in this situation?

In that split-second, a window in my mind opened to

reveal a memory. Not my own, but one belonging to Sharayah. She'd been staying the night in Sadie's private dorm room while Mauve had a "friend" over; she was lying on Sadie's couch, a thick textbook propped on her chest as she tried to study. But her eyelids felt heavy and the textbook even heavier, so she gave in to an afternoon nap. She was just settled into a relaxing sleep when Sadie entered the room.

Not in the mood to talk, Sharayah kept her eyes closed, feigning sleep. She listened to Sadie's footsteps, expecting her to flop onto her bed for a study session or tackle the homework on her desk. But the footsteps paused, then moved in the opposite direction—toward the couch.

Everything I saw, heard and felt came from inside Sharayah's body, as if we'd merged together in memory. Together we lay still, listening to Sadie's soft breaths, so curious now we peeked through the wispy hairs covering our face to watch Sadie bend over. When Sadie stood, I recognized the black purse in her hands—the same purse that I'd found a shocking amount of money in. Sadie snapped opened Sharayah's wallet. She chuckled softly as she flipped through green bills, plucking out a few and slipping them into her own pocket. And all the while Sharayah and I gritted our teeth, silently seething with wounded rage.

The memory faded to reality, yet I continued to sting with feelings of betrayal.

Sadie didn't just steal from stores.

She stole from her friends, too.

*

Despite this new insight into Sadie, I couldn't hate her. I wanted to—she definitely deserved it—but she was just so darned sweet. Besides, I was playing the role of Sharayah, who was aware of Sadie's thefts yet continued to hang out with her.

"How do you feel about Mexican?" Sadie asked as she started the car engine and waited to merge onto the street.

I shrugged, not really caring. I should have been hungry, but body-jumping had my inner system out of whack and it was hard to gauge ordinary things like appetite. "Whatever you want to eat is fine."

"Except sushi," she teased.

"Definitely not that," I said, unable to resist smiling back.

Minutes later, we pulled into a parking lot surrounded by palm trees and entered a crowded, adobe-style restaurant with a cactus theme both inside and outside.

My real body loved a variety of food in large amounts. Bean burritos, tacos, enchiladas ... hmmm. And once I got a spicy whiff, a volcano of appetite burst inside me and I ate breakfast, lunch, dinner and every meal for tomorrow. Afterwards, I was so stuffed I could hardly move or keep my eyes open. All I wanted was to curl up in a warm bed and sleep. So when we returned to the car and Sadie slipped into the driver's seat, I begged her to take me back to our so-called condo.

"You actually want to go back to the crappo condo?"

"Where else would we spend the night? On the beach?"

"That could be fun," she teased. "But I'm hoping for something much more interesting."

"Like what?" I asked cautiously.

"Mauve hinted she'll stay with Alonzo, at the house he

rented with Warren and some other friends. I'm planning on seeing a lot more of Warren, too."

"No! Not him!" I exclaimed before I could edit myself.

"Why not?" Sadie turned to me with a dangerous glint to her eyes. "Are you after Warren for yourself?"

"The total opposite." I shook my head emphatically. "I don't want you to get hurt by going off with some guy you barely know."

"So says the girl wearing a guy's shirt last night."

"That's not the same…"

"You're such a hypocrite—but your concern for me is sweet. Only trust me—I know what I'm doing with Warren." The light turned green and Sadie hit the gas pedal hard, jolting us forward.

"Be careful," I told her.

"I'm always a careful driver."

But I wasn't talking about driving.

Sighing, I leaned against the seat and closed my eyes.

"Don't you dare go to sleep now," Sadie said, slapping my shoulder. "We have a big night ahead of us. You need to find some guy for yourself, then none of us will have to stay in the crappo condo."

"I don't care where I sleep as long as it happens soon."

"It's not even seven yet!" Sadie complained. "It's like a law that we have to party till the morning on our first night of spring break."

"I'll pass. I'm too tired."

"Who are you? And what have you done with the real Sharayah?"

Shock ripped through me. Had she guessed my secret?

Then Sadie grinned and I realized she'd been joking.

"Please, please, please Rayah, come with me tonight," she persisted. "It won't be as fun without you—and there's going to be karaoke."

"So?"

"You *love* karaoke! And I love rooting for you from the audience. After you sing everyone always tells me you should be on American Idol. You could be as famous as Mariah or Britney if you had the guts to go out and make it big."

I smiled to myself, thinking of the *Voice Choice* contest.

Still, I shook my head. "I'm too wiped to go anywhere tonight."

"Since when do you choose sleeping over partying? Oh, I get it now." Sadie gave me a look oozing with sympathy. "Here I'm rattling on about my new guy when yours is back in San Jose. Are you missing James?"

"Who?" I furrowed my brow. "Oh! James."

Sadie reached across the seat to give me a playful slap on my arm. "You really must be tired if you can't remember your boyfriend's name."

"Completely exhausted," I said with a yawn.

"Would you be better if you called him? Use my phone."

"Thanks," I said, jumping at this opportunity.

When she handed me the phone, I pretended I was calling James (who I wouldn't recognize if he plopped down in my lap!), but covertly checked for voice or text messages from Eli. Unfortunately, there were none. And when I tried his number again, I got his voicemail. Damn, what was going on with him?

"No luck," I told Sadie as I returned her phone. "But I'm

too tired to talk anyway. I can hardly lift the phone. I'll be good to go tomorrow."

"I'll hold you to that. I'll cover for you when I see everyone." She stared out the windshield and gave a dreamy sigh. "It'll be so great to see Warren again."

She went on to talk about...you guessed it! Warren. Whenever she said his name, my stomach knotted and I wished I could warn her. But if I told her about Warren attacking me, she'd either accuse me of lying or leading him on. Sharayah had a track record when it came to stealing other girls' boyfriends.

Besides, I needed to stay on Sadie's good side to succeed at my mission. A big part of my plan to make Sharayah a singing star involved getting a ride to the audition in Beverly Hills. If Eli showed up, he could take me. But I couldn't count on that. If I didn't hear from him by tomorrow, I'd need to resort to Plan B—which meant not pissing off Sadie so she'd drive me to the audition.

Under the flicker of a short-circuiting street light and the gloom of a misty night, the crappo condo was even less inviting. There were no lights except a dim glow through the living room window, which added to the whole haunted house effect of the sagging porch, the peeling paint and the glass-eyed attic window peeking down at us like a spying ghost.

Fortunately, I had a good relationship with the other side; dead people didn't scare me.

Our arms full of luggage and shopping bags, we went inside, kicking a box out of the way and walking over a pile of dirty clothes. Sadie found a note on the fridge instructing us to sleep in the room at the far end of the hallway. Not a luxury room with a view of the ocean, but it seemed decent. A queen-sized bed with a flowered comforter and four matching pillows took up most of the space, while an uncomfortable-looking rollaway was folded against a wall. There were two dressers, a desk, a glassed-door curio case filled with ceramic cats, and several framed paintings of cats adorning the walls. As a cat lover, I was completely at ease with the kitty decor. All I cared about was going to sleep ... the bed looked so inviting.

Dropping my suitcase, I started for the bed.

Sadie grabbed my arm. "Not yet—there could be icky germs all over that. Wait until I clean up in here. I've got sheets, pillow cases and cleaning fluids."

"You bought all of that today?" I asked, seriously impressed.

"That and more."

"Impressive. You think of everything."

"I try," she said proudly. "Remember that, next time you call me a shopaholic."

"Me? Criticize your shopping obsession?" I teased. "Never happens."

"Yeah, right. And it's not an obsession, it's a talent. Check out what I bought."

Sadie was showing me cleaning liquids and bedding when suddenly a sleek, multicolored creature shot out from underneath the bed and pounced on her lap.

Swearing, Sadie shot at least a foot off the ground.

The cat tumbled down, landing expertly on its four feet.

"A cat!" Sadie reached down to pick up a bottle of cleaner that had rolled out of her bag. "Who let it into our room?"

"It's the other way around. I think this is her room and

we're the invaders." I laughed as the calico turned its back on us and curled cozily between the two bed pillows. "I don't think she has any intention of leaving."

"Just great. We'll have cat fur all over our clothes and I'll need to take—" she sneezed "—an allergy pill."

"You're allergic to cats?"

"Duh, you know I am. Cats, dogs, ferrets, people with bad hygiene." She rubbed her eyes. "And you can bet my cousin knows, too. She did this on purpose! Everything about this place has been a disaster! If all the hotels around here weren't booked, I'd so check into one right now."

"Hotels are really expensive," I pointed out.

"So I'd just charge it. Or you can pay. Do you have any extra hundred-dollar bills lying around?"

She asked this in a joking tone, but her words startled me. I almost answered, "Yes, I happen to have a big wad of hundreds in my purse." But I swallowed the idea of honesty and fought to hide my panic. Did she know about the hidden money? And why was Sharayah carrying around so much cash anyway—especially after discovering Sadie's five-fingered habit? It seemed so reckless, as if she was daring Sadie to steal from her again.

While I was burdened with guilt and secrets, Sadie didn't even notice. "There's no way I can sleep in a room covered in cat hair," she said, scowling at the sleeping cat.

"So, where . . . " I yawned " . . . will you sleep?"

"If things don't work out with Warren, I'll crash in the car."

I tried to listen as I flopped onto the bed, but my brain had already checked out. Sleep, blissful sleep, that's all I craved . . . I was only slightly aware of Sadie fixing her hair and changing into a clingy, night-black dress. I was glad when she left—relieved to be blissfully alone.

Well, except for the cat. She (I'd already guessed it was a "she," since male calicos are rare) peeked out from her plush cave between pillows, a splash of white fur under her orange nose. Her large green eyes studied me, and her orange tail swished across my face, tickling. When I didn't push her away, and instead scratched gently under her soft neck, she purred. She curled on my chest; her soft, warm fur-body pressed up against me was actually very nice. Closing my eyes, I imagined being at home with my own cat, resting in my bedroom with my parents just a shout away and my little sisters toddling around the house.

These memories were a sweet lullaby, carrying me deep into sleep. I only stirred once, to move my hand when it was being kitty-kissed by a rough tongue.

I don't know how long I was deep asleep before I heard hissing, spitting, and growling.

Something heavy pounced at the edge of the bed.

Bolting upright, I gaped around the darkened room. It was dimly lit by a slice of moonlight shining through the curtain slits. Beside me, the orange cat continued to hiss at the murky shape, her back arched, her ears flattened back, and her fur raised in attack mode.

Following her gaze, I saw a beast twice the size of the cat.

Fierce sharp teeth, gleaming.

At me.

14

I started to scream—then snapped my mouth shut.

My eyes adjusted to the dark, and I realized that it wasn't the beast's teeth that were gleaming but the shimmering collar around its neck. Not an ordinary collar, either, but a Duty Director: a glowing, otherworldly sphere spinning with holographic images. The beast was just a dog, with black curly fur, floppy ears and a happy-to-see you wagging tail. When I was a little girl he'd been my constant companion—until he died at a ripe old age.

"Cola!" I cried, startling the cat. Hissing, she scampered off the bed and disappeared. "I'm so glad to see you!"

What sounded like an ordinary bark translated inside my head to, *I came because I heard you were having problems.*

"Am I ever! I lost the GEM and can't find out anything about my mission. It's driving me crazy, trying to live someone else's life without knowing much about them. I did figure stuff out, though, and I have a plan to help her."

That's no longer your concern.

"Of course it is. Before I lost the GEM, I read the Nine Divine Rules so I know that part of my job is to guide my Host Body to better choices."

Secrecy is also part of your job, Cola said disapprovingly.

"I didn't know that until after I'd already told Eli." I didn't add that Eli hadn't kept the secret, either. "But since I read the GEM rules I've been following through on Sharayah's plans and I haven't gotten any tattoos or piercings. I've even figured out how to help Sharayah. There's an audition in two days—"

You won't be here in two days. Cola's dark eyes shone at me.

"Why not?" I asked nervously.

Your grandmother has reconsidered your mission.

"What do you mean?"

Your grandmother is sorry for all your troubles and regrets sending you on this mission without training or experience. She apologizes for her mistake.

"But it wasn't a mistake—I've been helping Sharayah."

Arrangements have been made to reverse the soul exchange. You will return to your physical body tomorrow.

"Tomorrow!" I cried, shaking my head.

Isn't that quick enough? Do you need to switch sooner?

"No! That's not it at all! I'm not ready to go back."

Cola cocked his head, looking less like an angelic messenger and more like an ordinary dog given a command he doesn't understand. *You don't want to return to your true body?*

"Sure I do—just not till after the audition. It'll boost Sharayah's singing career and her self-esteem. This guy, Gabe, broke her heart and destroyed her spirit so much she gave up on herself. Now do you understand why I can't leave?"

No. But I am only a messenger—your grandmother is the boss.

"Then give her a message that I need to stay for two more days."

It will do no good. She wants you away from danger.

"Danger?" Squeezing my pillow to my chest, I glanced quickly around the shadowy room. "What are you talking about?"

A Dark Lifer has been reported in the area.

"I knew it! I've been suspicious of Warren ever since I met him. No one wears gloves to the beach unless they have something to hide. But how did you find out?"

Cola's Duty Director started flashing red and green lights as it began to spin. *There are Earthbounders—humans like you—who are sensitive to energy shifts.*

"Do you mean psychics?" I guessed.

That's one of the words to describe those with this ability. Some of them work for us—reporting unusual activity. So you've met this Dark Lifer?

"Yes," I admitted. "Warren tricked me to going with him to a deserted building and I think he would have attacked me if he wasn't interrupted."

Cola's response was an angry growl that was probably the same as swearing in mental dog-language.

"I wasn't hurt," I said quickly, to calm him down. "I got away before he could take off his gloves and steal my energy."

When he is captured, he will be punished severely. Cola lifted his black nose, sniffing close to me. *This explains the foul odor around you.*

"You can smell a Dark Lifer on me?" I asked, surprised (and a little embarrassed) as I sat up straighter, tucking my legs beneath me.

What sort of dog would I be if I couldn't detect the foul essence of a Dark Lifer? Cola said, sounding insulted.

"Do I stink now?" I asked him.

Not to other humans, but it's revolting to me. He scooted back to the edge of the bed.

"Sorry." I sniffed myself, smelling nothing out of the ordinary.

My sniffer is so highly trained that even secondhand Dark Lifer odors are unpleasant. Still, out of loyalty to your grand-mother, I do occasional tracking for her. I'll need a description of the Dark Lifer.

"Warren is really muscular and—"

Not that kind of description. Cola moved closer to me, his Duty Director bursting with lights in dazzling rainbow hues. The colors merged in a brilliant iridescence as it whirled; it was spinning so fast it made me dizzy. It changed, too, lengthening and lifting, slipping over Cola's floppy ears and rising above his head like an airship poised to launch into space.

But instead of flying away, it sailed toward me and hovered right on top of my head, sending a gush of energized wind over me so soft and sweet it felt like a shower of air kisses. Instinctively I reached up to touch the collar, but a shocking electric tingle zapped my fingers. I pulled back, startled but not hurt.

Sit, my dog commanded, an edge of irritation in his mind-tone.

"Why? What's happening up there?" I pointed to the space above my head.

The Duty Director is preparing to scan your memories.

"Will it hurt?"

You won't feel anything as it accesses the information. Sit, and stay still.

I obeyed my dog, which seemed an ironic role reversal. Sitting cross-legged on the bed, I held my back straight and my head high as the Duty Director whirled over me like a fan and Cola studied me with his black, shining eyes. It was all so weird and surreal—sitting in a stranger's bed, chatting with my dead dog in a bedroom decorated with kitty pictures.

It's ready now, Cola mind-spoke. *When did you last see the Dark Lifer?*

"Today." I glanced at a clock. "I mean, yesterday."

Where were you when you saw him?

Easy enough. I thought back to the dark warehouse where bicycles surrounded the walls and Warren blocked the way to the door. Warren's hands, concealed in leather, had been reaching for me, so dangerously close that remembering made me hot with fear about what might have happened.

Got it! Good girl! Cola's voice applauded.

The whistling over my head stilled as the whirling collar floated away from me and circled quietly in the air.

"You're done? Already?" Cautiously reaching up, I touched my head. "What exactly did you do?"

Copied the live image of the Dark Lifer from your memories. Then the Duty Director distributed the images to members of the Dark Disposal Team to aid in the capture of the renegade soul.

I nodded, remembering my experience with the DDT— how a man and woman wearing ordinary business suits appeared out of nothingness and captured a dangerous Dark Lifer with their snake-like silver ropes. Then, in a flash, they were gone, taking their prisoner with them.

"So they'll get rid of Warren?" I asked hopefully.

They'll try—knowing his temporary appearance helps. Most Dark Lifers are confused souls who run because they're afraid. They are easy to apprehend. The one you came in contact with last week was like that.

"His capture was quick," I agreed.

That's the way it is with most Dark Lifers. But then there are the old souls, the Dark Lifers who have been switching bodies for centuries and are clever and elusive.

"Warren didn't seem very clever when he was running from a knife," I scoffed.

He had reason to be afraid. If a borrowed body is injured and bleeds the Dark Lifer inside is ejected and has only ten minutes to find a new body before the DD Team discovers his (or her) location. Without the protection of a human body, souls shine so brightly they can be seen from the other side. Even a newbie Dark Lifer would know to run from a knife.

"But if Dark Lifers can hide in human bodies, how do you find them?"

Eighty percent of Dark Lifers are frightened after a few days hiding in a borrowed body and they beg to be returned. Nineteen percent are easily caught because they make dumb mistakes that draw attention to themselves.

Math from my dead dog. Go figure.

"What about the other one percent?" I asked curiously.

That's the hard part. If they suspect we're closing in on them, they switch to a new body. Cola puffed out a doggy sigh. *There is only one sure way to catch them.*

"How?"

Deception. The Dark Disposal Team must catch them unaware—but this is difficult without the help of a living person.

"I'm alive—and I'd like to help," I offered. "If Warren isn't caught soon, he'll go after my friend Sadie. I'll do whatever I can to stop him."

I cannot allow that. Risking your body is against the Divine Rules. If this Dark Lifer is an old soul, he may have the strength and knowledge to drain your energy until you can't even breathe. The lucky ones die.

"Die! You mean really die…like you and Grammy Greta?"

Worse. We ended long lives naturally and made it to the other side safely with healthy souls.

"What happens to the 'unlucky' ones?"

Insanity—they lose their minds. Cola pointed a furry paw at me. *Besides, your grandmother would never allow it.*

"So don't tell her."

I would never go against her orders—and warn you not to, either. For your soul's safety, stay away from Dark Lifers.

Then Cola slipped his Duty Director back on and vanished.

15

Despite my utter exhaustion, I slept badly that night. Tossing, turning, tormented, my thoughts spun into tornadoes of confusion. I was torn between wanting to return to my real body and wanting to stay in Sharayah's body long enough to get her to the audition. If I could jump-start her career, that would help fix all her problems. I had to show her she was worth more than some guy who broke her heart, and that she had the talent to become a star. She needed to stop throwing herself at random guys and return to her family. Being admired by fans was a great cure for heartbreak. She'd be so busy she'd forget all about Gabe. And Eli would get his sister back.

Grammy was wrong about my being wrong for the mission.

No matter what it took, I'd prove that I wasn't a failure. I could handle a Temp Lifer mission just as well as a dead soul could.

Still, as I slipped in and out of dreams, I thought of my family and friends and how much I missed them. Drifting on memories, I relived a perfect day where everyone I cared about came together to celebrate a triple birthday.

If days could be rated, this one deserved a Ten-Plus-Perfect. Everyone I cared about was there—my parents, sisters, best friends, neighbor Dilly, my cousin Zeke (minus Aunt Suzanne), all smiling and having a great time. The ice cream was even my favorite flavor—Heavenly Hash.

When I woke up, the taste of ice cream lingered in my mouth and a tear trailed down my cheek.

Sitting up in bed, still wearing yesterday's clothes, I was alone except for the cat curled beside me. I scooped her furry body into my arms, struggling against an overwhelming wave of loneliness.

"I miss everyone so much, Kitty Calico," I whispered. "But I can't go back yet."

Only how could I convince Grammy?

I really needed to talk to someone—and not just anyone, but the one person who knew all my secrets and understood me better than anyone else: my best friend forever, Alyce. I could always count on her to listen without interrupting while I vented, and to assure me everything would be okay. Whenever I was a mopey mess of emotions, I'd vent to Alyce and she'd know the perfect thing to say to make me feel better. But lately (since my near-death and body-switching), we hadn't had a chance for a heart-to-heart talk.

Well, why not now?

A surge of hope sent me flying off the bed, causing a meow of complaint from Kitty Calico, who skittered out of my way as I hurried out of the room.

I searched all over until I finally found a phone (one of those old fashioned ones with a dial, if you can believe it!) perched on a shelf in the bathroom. I called the familiar number (making a mental note to leave money to pay for the call). Then I crossed my fingers on both hands, hoping that Alyce's mother had already left for work.

The finger-crossing worked!

"Who is this?" Alyce asked in such a sharp tone that I felt hurt until I remembered she wouldn't recognize my voice. Well, duh. I was still getting used to it myself.

"It's me!" I yipped with joy.

"And you are...?"

"—thrilled to finally talk to you!" I said in an excited rush. "I'm so glad you're there, although I wish you were here or that I was there with you, whatever works, just so we could talk together, even if it meant hanging out at gross graveyards so you can take more 'Morbidity' pictures for your photo journal."

Silence, then a gasp. "Amber?"

"Yeah, it's really me."

"But you sound so... so not you."

"I swear, underneath this college girl's body, I'm the same BFF that once dressed up like a vampire, dripped fake blood from my fake fangs and pretended to bite Dustin so you could take a picture for your collection."

"The photo turned out great. Ohmygod... Amber." Her voice cracked.

"Exactly," I said, delighted to be called by my real name. "You won't believe everything that's been going on."

"I know a little from Dustin, and he also told me what Eli said. I want to hear everything, but I can't talk here." She was whispering. "Wait while I go to my room so Mom can't hear."

"She's home? I thought she'd be at work."

"No … she called in sick." I heard the sound of a door shutting and then Alyce added, "I'm in my room now so we can talk freely. Where are you?"

"Venice Beach. At the crappo condo." I laughed wryly. "I'm here alone except for a calico cat. I don't know her name but she slept with me last night. Not that I was really able to sleep after a completely insane day. How much did Dustin tell you?"

"Only that your grandmother switched you into Eli's sister's body and you're in Venice Beach for spring break. Is that true?"

"As ridiculous as it sounds—yes." I proceeded to explain, not leaving out even the most embarrassing details like waking up wearing a guy's shirt, puking in a parking lot and strutting on stage for the wet T-shirt contest. I was always completely honest with Alyce, just like she was with me.

And in true Alyce form, she simply listened.

"Then last night Cola told me Grammy is pulling me off the mission," I griped. "How can she do that to me? My grandmother is more protective on the other side than she was when she was alive. She says it's too dangerous for me to stay in Sharayah's body. But it's more than that. I've failed her by losing the GEM—that's the instruction manual. And now I'm going to fail Sharayah, too. I really blew it this time, Alyce."

"You did your best. Sometimes things just don't work out."

"But I could *make* it work if I had more time." I sighed. "What am I going to do?"

"Come home," she said simply.

"Believe me—I want to!"

"Then do it."

"I can't go back as a failure." I groaned, twisting the phone cord through my fingers. "If I can convince Grammy to let me stay for the audition, everything will work out. Sharayah is the most incredible singer—better than any of those American Idols. Kelly Clarkson would be envious! Sharayah could be even more famous than her, unless she misses this big chance. If only Eli would show up with the GEM, then I could contact Grammy directly. Have you heard anything from Eli?"

"Why would your boyfriend call me?"

"I don't know ... I guess I'm just worried because he hasn't called me back. Of course he might have tried by now, only I won't know until I see Sadie again. And I have no idea how to find her or Mauve. And what's bothering me the most is not hearing from Eli." The phone cord was now wrapped so tight that it was starting to cut off circulation. I unwound it, my hand free, but my heart still tied up in knots. "I just don't know what to do. Alyce, what do you think?"

I waited for her encouragement, but there was a long pause.

"I think you should come home now. But you don't seem

to care what I say," she finally said, in a sharp, very un-BFF tone.

"Of course I care."

"You don't act like it."

"What's this about, Alyce?" I asked.

"Nothing," she snapped, in a way that definitely meant "something."

"Alyce, are you mad because last time, when I was in Leah's body, I didn't immediately tell you I wasn't dead? I've already explained that."

"Why does everything have to be about you?" Her hostility shocked me. Whenever I got too dramatic, she would tell me to cut it out and call me her nickname, "Dramber." But that was always done with a smile and good-natured teasing.

This time there was no teasing in her tone.

"I can't believe you said that," I told her, stung.

"That's because it never occurs to you that other people might have problems, too."

"Like you?" I asked, trying desperately to understand why she seemed so angry. "Is something wrong?"

"If it was, would you notice?" she retorted.

"Of course I would."

"Yet when I told you mom missed work you didn't even ask why. You never think about what I'm going through. A week ago I thought you were dead—do you have any idea how awful that was? I went around like a zombie, not able to sleep or eat or talk to anyone because you were the only one I wanted to talk to and you weren't here." Her voice cracked. "When we finally got to talk, I had to pretend like I hadn't gone through hell for a few days. But before we can have a real talk, you leave again and it's Dustin—not you—who tells me you've switched bodies."

"I called," I tried to explain. "Your mother said you were unavailable."

"But you called Eli first—a guy you've only just met—rather than me."

I couldn't argue because she was right. "I'm sorry."

"You're always sorry. I should be used to that by now and not expect any more. But lately I've felt so alone. "

"I can't read your mind. I had no idea you were upset."

"You don't pay attention." She made a soft sound like a sob. Alyce, crying? But she was the toughest person I knew, and never cried.

"I'm paying attention now. Talk to me, Alyce."

"I can't ... not over the phone. Come home ASAP."

"Grammy plans to switch me back today," I admitted. "But I want her to wait until tomorrow so I can go to the audition. I can't just quit on Sharayah when I'm so close to giving her chance at stardom. All I need is one more day."

"Sure, help her. Isn't that what you expect me to say?"

"I don't expect you to say anything but the truth."

"You don't want to hear the truth. I don't even know why you bothered to call me." Her voice broke. "Just go ... go have fun with new friends."

"Mauve and Sadie? That's ridiculous! I barely know them and they have no idea who I really am."

"Yet you're all having a great time together—dancing, flirting, hanging out on the beach. It's so interesting to hear you go on and on and *on* about them. Thanks for sharing."

"Alyce, don't! You're my only BFF and I'd rather be with you than anyone else. You know that."

"Do I?" Alyce asked quietly.

"I might be dense sometimes, but I never stop caring. I'll be home tomorrow—I promise. Then we'll have one of our Double A's talks. Just the two of us, like always."

"Yeah. Like always."

But the way she said "always" sounded like an accusation.

And before I could say anything else—even good-bye—she hung up.

✳

Only the heartbreak Sharayah had felt when Gabe tied her hands and called her a "fool" came close to the hurt I was feeling. Alyce and I'd had arguments before, but we'd always kept talking until we worked things out. Never—not once in all the years of our friendship—had she hung up on me.

I called Alyce back, but she didn't pick up. On purpose, I was sure, which hurt even more. How had this all happened? What sin had I committed to deserve so much anger? I thought back over the last week: that awful moment when I'd woken up in the first wrong body, terrified and unable to contact anyone. But I hadn't been the only one who'd suffered. I'd been so wrapped up in my own misery that I hadn't thought much about what my friends were going through. During that awful week, Alyce thought I was dying and visited my body in the hospital every day. She'd been a loyal friend, while what had I done for her? Let her think I was dead.

No wonder she was so angry.

I sucked at being a BFF.

And the only thing I could think of to make this up to her was to come home today.

I really, really hated quitting on Sharayah—but Alyce was my best friend ever and came first. She needed me.

Decision made.

Walking back into the bedroom, I plopped my suitcase on the bed. I found a tie-dyed T-shirt and slipped it over jeans. Then I packed yesterday's dirty clothes in a side pouch and got ready to leave.

Mentally, I went through a checklist of my options.

There was no point in trying to contact Sadie and Mauve. I'd just leave them a note explaining I had to go home for a family emergency. I wouldn't be lying. Alyce was closer than family to me.

I'd use Sharayah's money and take a taxi to the airport, then catch the first plane home. If everything worked out, I'd be with Alyce by this afternoon. Then we'd talk and I'd find out what was really bothering her. While I knew she was upset about my being temporarily dead, I doubted that was the core problem. No, it was something deeper … and I'd help her get through whatever it was.

The cat mewed, jumping off the bed to rub against my legs.

"Bye, Kitty Calico," I said softly.

Then I grabbed my suitcase and rolled it out of the room.

In the kitchen, I found a pen on a counter but no paper for a "good-bye" note, so I ripped off a square of paper towel. I wrote a short good-bye to Sadie and Mauve, apologizing for cutting my vacation short and promising to explain later. (Not the truth, of course, but something close enough to satisfy them.)

When I reached the living room, I sorted through a thick pile of phone books (a few so old they were dated back to the last millennium) and thumbed through the yellow pages for "taxi." The dispatcher said a taxi would arrive in thirty minutes. I picked up my suitcase and, with a heavy sigh, reached for the door and opened it...

And was startled by someone walking up the porch steps.

Eli had arrived.

16

"You!" I shrieked, dropping my suitcase with a thud on the hardwood floor.

"Amber? Is it you?" He tilted his head uncertainly.

"Yes! It's me ... and it's you ... here! I can't believe it! I've never been happier to see anyone!"

Rushing at him, I opened my arms, ready to show exactly how much I missed him—but instead of opening his arms for me, he folded them across his chest, his expression repulsed like I had lice or smelled bad.

"No," he said firmly. "I can't touch you."

"Why not?" I demanded, stung.

"Because I can't." He frowned. "Amber, any touching would be wrong. You're not you anymore."

"Of course I am. So what if I look different?"

"You're more than different. You look like my sister. You *are* my sister."

"Damn. I forgot about that." I glanced down at myself. "So I guess kissing is out."

"So far out the idea just left the planet. Sorry, but that's just how I feel. It's not that I don't want to . . . well, you know."

"It's okay. I understand." I was smiling a little because he seemed so disappointed. It was cute how he was so serious, frowning as if all the problems of the world had been dropped on his shoulders. He really did care about me.

Picking up my suitcase, Eli walked me into the house and shut the door behind us. He stared at me, then slowly smiled. "I think it would be okay if we shook hands," he said.

"Are you sure that's allowed?"

He nodded. "Platonically."

"Of course," I agreed as I held out my hand.

The casual shake felt far from casual and rocked my emotions. Eli must have felt some of that rocking, too, because as if in silent agreement we immediately dropped hands and stepped back. I glanced everywhere except at him, noticing a loose spring on the couch, a broken TV that had been turned into a planter with green vines dangling among loose wires, and a light switch on the wall that had been transformed into modern art by an abstract painter.

When I found the courage to lift my eyes, Eli was staring at my suitcase with a puzzled expression. "Are you going somewhere?"

I nodded. "I was going to the airport to fly home."

"Why? Aren't you supposed to stay here for spring break?"

"Change of plans: my mission is over."

"That's great! My family will be so relieved when Sharayah returns and everything is back to normal."

"I hope so," I said, guiltily because nothing had been solved and I had no idea how Sharayah would act when she resumed her life. But Eli seemed so happy, I didn't want to worry him.

"I'm glad this is ending for other reasons, too," Eli added, biting his lower lip as he met my gaze. "I look at you and see my sister—which is really messed up. Once you're not her anymore, we can do more than shake hands. Oh, I didn't mean that the way it sounded. Geez, I'm not that kind of guy."

"I know exactly what kind of guy you are—my kind." I lightly touched his arm. "And when this is all over I'd love to go out with you."

"It's a date," he said, nodding.

I nodded, too, feeling tingly all over. I really, really wanted to kiss him.

But I could wait.

"I don't understand why you're going to the airport." Eli rubbed his chin, giving me a puzzled look.

"What do you mean?"

"Won't the body change happen wherever you are? So why not leave Sharayah here to enjoy her vacation?"

"I have to get home ASAP so I can talk to Alyce. She needs me today. And since I don't know exactly when the change will happen, I'm flying home immediately. A taxi will be here soon."

"Cancel it," Eli said firmly.

"I can't." My throat tightened as I remembered Alyce's accusations. "I have to fix things with Alyce."

"Still, you don't need a taxi to get to the airport. I can drive you."

"You'd do that for me?"

"I drove all the way here, didn't I?"

"Yes." I met his gaze. "You did."

He met my gaze with such honesty that I trusted him completely.

After I cancelled the taxi, we cleared a space on the couch and sat down to talk. The house was quiet, without even the scamper of kitty feet.

"Interesting place you're staying in." Eli's lips curled with amusement as he gestured at the mismatched furniture, boxes and other oddities scattered around the room. "Not exactly a five-star hotel."

"More like a no-star hovel. But it came with a cat, so I can't complain."

"I didn't know you liked cats."

"We have one at home, part Siamese and all attitude. And I love dogs, too," I said fondly, thinking of Cola.

"Cats, dogs … I'm a fan of almost all animals," he said.

"Almost? What animals don't you like?"

"Well … it's kind of embarrassing to admit."

I pantomimed zipping my lips. "I won't tell. What?"

"Birds—they freak me out. My grandpa had this mean parrot once that bit my ear. I was only four, but that kind of pain you don't forget. I still have a scar right here," he added, pointing to his left ear.

I leaned closer to look at the tiny jagged white scar on his ear lobe, aware of the few inches between us and careful not to accidentally caress him with his sister's hands. It was safe to talk about animals and not about what was really on our minds.

But it was time to get serious.

"Eli, did you bring it?" I asked quietly.

He knew exactly what I meant and reached into his coat pocket. "Here," he said, handing me a small book.

I took my GEM, frowning a little because now that I finally had it there was no need to use it. My mission was over—whether I wanted it to be or not. Still, it felt good to hold my tiny link to the other side.

"Thanks for bringing it all this way," I told Eli.

"I said I would—although getting here hasn't been easy."

"I wondered why you didn't call me back."

"Sorry," he said sheepishly. "I wanted to but I couldn't. Remember the girl from the dorm I told you about who was helping me?"

How could I forget? Gritting my teeth I said, "Yeah. Kate-lyn."

"Well it turns out we have the same cell phone model—and she took mine by mistake. So I didn't get your message with your address until she realized the mistake and called me. By then, I had other problems. Dad was mad that I hadn't returned right home with the car he loaned me, and he ordered me to 'haul my ass home or else.'"

"Did you go home?"

"You bet—no one defies Dad. I'd already disappointed him by refusing to work at the car lot and I didn't want to make things worse. Besides, going home gave me a chance to talk to Mom. She's been so worried about Sharayah."

For good reason, I thought grimly.

"When I told her I was trying to help Sharayah, she was thrilled," Eli continued. "I don't know what she told Dad, but next thing I knew he was handing me the keys to a brand new car and slipping me a credit card for gas. I finally got a call from Katelyn, who explained the phone mix-up, and once I had the address I drove right here."

"Thanks so much—especially for my GEM." I rubbed my hand over the smooth cover. "Although it's not much use to me now."

"Are you sure?" he asked, frowning. "There could be information in it that would help Sharayah. What will happen to her when you switch back?"

"She'll resume her own life."

"But will she be okay?"

I wanted to answer "yes," but the intuitive connection I shared with Sharayah told me otherwise. Her fragile soul, sleeping in my physical body, was getting a needed rest, but that was only a Band-Aid on a much deeper wound. She needed to get over Gabe's cruelty and regain her self-confidence.

Unfortunately, I could no longer help her.

Still, Eli was right about there being no rush for me to get to the airport. In fact, why get on a plane at all? I could travel on more mysterious planes. All I had to do was wait for Grammy to return me to my own body. In a blink of a soul switch, I'd travel over 400 miles and I'd wake up in a hospital bed. Once I was myself again, I'd go right to Alyce and stay with her all night if that's what it took to mend our friendship.

"Aren't you going to open it up?" Eli asked, gesturing toward the book.

"No," I said wryly. "My mission is over."

"Not officially. You're still my sister."

"For a few hours, anyway—which isn't long enough to finish my job. I totally messed up as a Temp Lifer."

"You did your best in a crazy situation. And after the switch, I'll stick around here to help my sister. Your insider information will make it easier to convince her to come back home with me."

"But she can't go home until after the *Voice Choice* audition tomorrow," I insisted. "You have to get her there—and arrive early because there will probably be a long line."

"I will," Eli promised. "Even if it means kidnapping her."

"Don't cause her to scream—that's terrible for her vocal chords."

He stared at me uneasily. "You're kidding … right?"

I fixed him with a dead-serious look, then relaxed into a grin. "Of course I'm kidding. Besides, you shouldn't have any trouble convincing Sharayah. You're her brother, she'll listen to you."

"Her *younger* brother. Usually she's the one telling me what to do, not the other way around."

"Oh. Then I better consult the GEM for advice." I looked down at the small book. "I'll find out what we should do about the audition and whether the DD Team caught the Dark Lifer."

"What Dark Lifer?" Eli nearly jumped off the couch.

"Oh, didn't I tell you about him?"

"No, you did not," he said accusingly.

I wasn't eager to talk about what had happened, but Eli had done so much for me, I owed him the truth. So I told him everything—except about my rescue by Dyce. Somehow that seemed like a bad idea.

"Anyway, it's all over now," I finished. "The DD Team will get rid of the dead guy hiding out in Warren."

"What about the real Warren? What happens to him?"

"I don't really know. I guess he'll be okay. He'll probably wake up with confused memories but blame it on partying too hard."

"Poor guy," Eli sympathized. "It reminds me of a corny movie about zombies and body snatching. Yet it's really happening and Dark Lifers seem to be stalking you."

"Maybe they still are," I said with growing trepidation. Holding out the GEM, I flipped it open, not surprised this time to find only blank paper. But I knew what to do.

"GEM, could you tell me about the Dark Lifer in Warren?" I asked. "Has he been captured yet?"

As I stared at the paper, it changed, rippling with movement like stiff fingers stretching, then growing so bright it seemed to glow.

A single word curled across the page in perfect cursive penmanship.

No.

"He hasn't?" My heart skipped. "Why not?"

Unable to locate the Dark Lifer.

"But I told Cola he was staying in Venice Beach. If Cola could smell his essence on me, why can't the DDT find him?"

An exact location is required.

"He's staying in a beach house with his friend Alonzo. I don't know the address."

Find out.

"How am I supposed to do that?" I retorted. "I'm just a rookie Temp Lifer who messed up my first real assignment. What do you expect from me? A miracle?"

A three-letter word flashed across the page—large, bold, and demanding.

YES.

Then, without my even touching the book, it slammed itself shut.

"Why'd you close it already?" Eli asked, peering over my shoulder. "We haven't asked for advice on how to help my sister."

"The book has ideas of its own," I said, a little annoyed at being ordered around by a bunch of paper. "But I'll ask it about your sister afterwards."

He furrowed his brow. "After what?"

"After we go to the beach." I tucked the GEM into my pocket. Grammy and Cola may have warned me not to get involved, but as a Temp Lifer, I had to obey the GEM.

"Why the beach?" Eli asked, following me to the door.

I couldn't help but smile. "Apparently I'm still on the job."

✳

Spring Break: Day Two.

Traffic insanity, pedestrians swarming the sidewalks, surfers in black wetsuits and rainbows of bikinis everywhere. And the action at the beach was even crazier. Finding a Dark Lifer was like trying to spot a minnow in the deep sea.

Unfortunately, I lacked Cola's sniffing talent.

"What does this dude look like?" Eli asked, because of course he'd insisted on coming with me even though I'd warned him that it could be dangerous. And I wasn't just referring to the Dark Lifer, I thought privately as I stared at hot, tanned girls showing lots of skin and curves. Eli was only in high school and too trusting. I'd have to stay close to protect him from any bikini-clad predators.

"Warren is blond, with big muscles and an ever bigger ego," I explained. "He wears leather gloves."

"Gloves? Weird."

"Exactly." I nodded. "I think he's hiding gray fingernails and glowing hands."

"It'll still be hard to find him with so many people hanging out on the beach."

"He and Alonzo will probably be hanging with Sadie and Mauve. Sadie is petite with long black braids and Mauve has bright pink hair so she should be easy to—there she is!"

"Mauve!" I called, running toward the beacon-pink hair.

She was sitting on a beach towel, smoothing sunscreen over her skin while staring off at a volleyball game where all the players were (a) male (b) bronzed (c) beach-a-liciously hot.

"Hey, Rayah," Mauve said lazily as she closed the lid on the sunscreen. "Guess you survived the crappo condo—or did you find somewhere else to stay?" Her gaze drifted to Eli.

Catching her drift, I firmly shook my head. "No!"

"No reason to get all defensive." She giggled. "So what if he's a little young? He's kind of cute and—"

"—my brother."

"Oh ... well, that explains why he looks so familiar." She lay down on her stomach, grinning up at us. "He's grown up a lot since the family portrait. So are you going to introduce us?"

"Mauve, this is Eli."

Eli nodded, blushing as if suddenly shy with an older, pretty girl. "Nice to meet you," he murmured.

"Cute and polite, obviously you're nothing like your sister." Mauve smirked knowingly. "So what brings you here, Eli? Did your parents send you to spy on Rayah?"

"I came down to visit some friends." Eli's gaze drifted to Mauve's hands as she worked the suntan lotion deeper into her thighs. He was a guy, after all, so I couldn't blame him for noticing. Mauve wasn't exactly a prim-and-proper girl next door; she was closer to a girl-going-for-anything-wild.

This was getting us nowhere and wasting time.

"Mauve, have you seen Warren?" I folded my arms across my chest, impatient to get moving.

"You just missed him. He went with Sadie and Alonzo to watch the sand-sculpture contest. They wanted me to go, but I'm working on my tan. The contest is over that way." She gestured far down the beach, where the dark mass of a crowd gathered near the shore.

Without giving Mauve a chance to ask any questions, I tugged on Eli's hand and headed off down the beach. I heard his sneakers slapping the sand so knew he was following. The sun was brighter today, with fewer clouds and no wind so the air seemed thick and muggy. Sweat dripped down my forehead and underarms as I hurried forward.

"What's the plan?" Eli asked, falling into step beside me.

"I find Warren and then pass on his location through the GEM, which is right here in my jeans pocket." The jeans were heavy and warm but the pockets came in handy and gave me the freedom not to carry a purse. "I just hope the DD Team responds quickly so that once I find Warren, he can't get away."

"Be careful around him," Eli cautioned.

"I will." I thought of the tomb-like bicycle warehouse, shuddering.

Glancing over at Eli, I considered telling him more about my scary encounter with Warren. But I had a feeling he might go all macho and do something stupid if he knew everything. And I had a guilty reluctance to say anything about Dyce. Eli might get the wrong idea about that, too.

It wasn't like we could talk much anyway, since the sound of shouts and conversation were getting louder as we neared the crowd surrounding the sand-sculpture contest. There were large, sectioned-off areas with groups working together—and fast—to shape damp sand into museum-worthy creations. By tomorrow the sand sculptures would wash away, as if their lives were temporary, too.

Passing a group of little boys making a sand pirate ship, I heard music nearby and followed the sound to a group of spring breakers dancing on the beach. I saw Alonzo first, sitting on the sand and gazing out at the ocean. He looked up with a start when I interrupted his meditation, then pointed toward the impromptu dance floor. In the midst of the gyrating bodies, Sadie and Warren bumped and swayed with such abandon that I suspected they'd started drinking early, or had never stopped and were continuing from last night.

It was creepy being near Warren again, and even creepier seeing his dragon gloves. Didn't he ever take them off? He had to realize he would stand out with such a peculiar style.

"Is that him?" Eli shouted close to my ear.

I nodded, pushing back nervous fear that made me want to run in the opposite direction. But I was too close to helping the DD Team capture Warren to quit now. I may not have the time to solve Sharayah's problem, but I could do this and make my grandmother proud.

But Sadie's proximity to Warren was a problem. I had to get her out of the way before I contacted the DD Team.

"Sadie!" I called, but I could hardly hear myself over the rush of noise. She didn't even turn my way.

"I'm going to get her," I told Eli.

"No!" he shouted, loud enough for me to hear.

"But he might hurt her."

"Or you," Eli said. "I'll go get her."

"Wait. I know what to do," I said, although I wasn't sure he could hear me.

I shook my head and pointed to Sadie. Her braids were swinging like black ropes as she rocked to the rousing beat, slapping into anyone unlucky enough to be within her range.

Even Warren kept his distance, swaying his shoulders but keeping his tell-tale gloves close to his side.

Cola had warned me to stay away from Dark Lifers. Grammy wouldn't be happy if I got too close to Warren, either. Okay, I'd play by the rules.

So I reached into my pocket and pulled out the GEM.

Despite the noise of ocean and music, when I opened the book and said I'd found the Dark Lifer, an excited rush of words streamed across the page.

Great work! DDT is on the way.

I'd hardly read the message before there was a startling flash.

Right in front of me, three people appeared: two men in business suits and a woman in a dignified, navy-blue skirt with a button-down white blouse. Surrounded by bikinis and casual jeans, they looked completely out of place. But only a few people seemed to notice them.

The woman bent close to me but didn't ask me any questions. She pointed to the GEM and then at me, her look focused with an intensity that made me a little dizzy.

Then the trio advanced on Warren, slim silver whips draped over their arms.

He was just bending his knees to boogie down to the sand when the DD Team surrounded him. Sadie kept dancing, waving her hands as she twirled. But Warren stopped dancing, jumping back like he'd been clawed by a sand crab. When the DD Team closed in on him, panic crossed his face.

But before they could lasso him with their silver ropes and take him back to the other side, Warren let out a scream and pushed past them.

Then he took off, running for his life ... his Dark Life.

17

"Warren! Come back!" Sadie cried, staring after him with dismay.

With the danger gone, I rushed over to her side and wrapped my arms around her. "Sadie! I'm so glad he didn't hurt you."

"Are you insane?" She pushed me away angrily. "Warren would never hurt me."

"Thank God he didn't get the chance!" I stared off down the beach where the running figures grew smaller, smaller... until they were only a smudge on the horizon. There was a glint of silver that could have been one of the ropes, and then nothing.

All four had vanished.

Sadie adjusted a shoulder strap of her bikini and wrapped a towel around her waist, covering the shiny red jewel in her belly piercing. With her hands on her hips, she glared at me. "What the hell is going on? And who are you?" She jabbed a finger at Eli.

"My brother. He just arrived."

"So ruining my life runs in your family." Sadie turned from us, staring off down the beach anxiously. "Is Warren going to come back? And who were those suits chasing him?"

"I really don't know."

"What do you know?" she demanded.

"Only that Warren was bad news," I said, raising my voice to be heard over the music. "I'll tell you what I know, but not here where I can hardly hear my own thoughts."

She nodded, complaining all the way from the beach to a shady area with benches. "This so sucks. Just when things are working out with Warren, these people show up and ruin everything. Warren was going to take me out tonight to a romantic, private resort."

"You wouldn't have liked it," I told her ominously.

"Says who? You're just jealous because I got Warren and you're hanging out with your little brother." Her words were sharp, but her lower lip quivered as we sat down on the cement bench farthest away from the jogging path. "Why did Warren run?"

Eli raised his brows at me as if to say, *What are you going to tell her?* I answered with a small head shake: *As if I know!* I ran all kinds of answers through my mind, but each one sounded more and more ridiculous. While I was racking my brain, Sadie's eyes welled up like she was going to cry ... but not because she was worried about Warren. She was worried all right—for herself. And I had a good idea why.

"Sadie, this might be hard to believe," I said carefully, placing my hand on her arm. "Those people after Warren were undercover cops."

"You're right—I don't believe it."

"It's true," Eli added.

She turned on him, glaring. "How do you know?"

"They showed us their badges when they questioned us." Eli sounded so convincing I almost believed him.

"You were questioned and didn't tell me?" Sadie exclaimed with an accusing look at me.

"Sworn to secrecy," I said gravely.

"Oh. My. God! This is ridiculous! Why are they after Warren?" She clutched her hands around her bead-fringed designer handbag. "What did he do?"

"Identity theft," Eli said.

"Shoplifting," I said at the same time.

"Which one?" Sadie demanded.

"Both," I replied before Eli could say something completely different.

"So everything he's told me...is a lie?" Sadie rubbed her reddening eyes. "Is his name even Warren?"

"Doubtful. He's had lots of names," I improvised. "Mark, Bradley and Alejandro were some I remember the police mentioning. That's why I warned you to stay away from him."

"But stealing isn't that big of a deal," Sadie insisted. "Everyone's done it at least once."

"Not everyone," Eli said.

Sadie put her hands on her hips and faced Eli skeptically. "Like you've never stolen anything?"

Eli shook his head. "Never."

"Not even from your parents? Not candy, money or a car?"

"Well ... " His shoulders sagged a little. "I've borrowed a car without asking a few times."

"Borrowing is just another word for stealing. So don't come off like you're better than Warren because he's made some mistakes. It's not fair how they chased him like some animal. What can they prove, anyway?"

"They've had him under surveillance since he used a stolen ATM card yesterday," I lied.

"Yesterday?" Sadie's mouth dropped open. "But I've been with Warren ... do you think they've been watching me, too?"

"Sure, but all you've done is hang out at the beach and the shops, so there's nothing to worry about. Right, Sadie?"

"Right," she said too quickly, gnawing on her pink-frosted thumb nail. She shifted her handbag to her shoulder and glanced down at the neon watch on her wrist. "I just remembered something I need to do."

"Shopping?" I guessed.

"No!" She shook her head, looking sick enough to vomit. "I may never shop again."

✳

Eli tilted his head curiously when Sadie raced off like she was being chased by the DD Team. "What's with her?" he asked.

But I just shrugged and said I didn't know. Even though I

wasn't really Sadie's friend, I felt loyal to her. And I had optimistic hopes that Sadie's conscience (or fear of tacky orange jail jumpsuits) would cause her to return stuff she stole and give up stealing forever. A book I'd read called *The Infernal Optimist* advised to always expect the best of people because they might surprise you by living up to your expectations.

We gazed back toward the ocean. The dancing had spread from the center of the beach all the way to the foaming shoreline, where barefoot spring breakers splashed and kicked up sand with the rise and fall of the surf. Due to the addition of a DJ and sound system, sound waves rivaled ocean waves, rocking powerfully enough to topple the sand sculptures. The people who weren't dancing were watching the dancing; no one seemed aware of the drama that had just taken place.

Except Eli and me.

We walked down to a rocky outcrop, where surf swirled into tide pools and tiny crabs scurried into sandy holes and dark crevices. We climbed across rocks until the music was muffled to a faraway buzz, drowned out by the rhythmic crashing waves and sea gulls shrieking as they wheeled and dived. Sitting down on a sandy patch of peacefulness tucked between rocks, we were both silent, wrapped in our own thoughts. I wondered what Eli was thinking; perhaps he was wondering the same thing about me. We'd been so focused on other-side problems that there hadn't been any time for us. Now that we did have time, there was an awkward silence.

"Well…" Eli finally said, glancing at me expectantly. "Now what happens?"

"I'm not sure. I could be switched back any minute."

He nodded, looking disappointed. I felt disappointed, too.

Here I was with the guy I maybe-loved, relaxing by the ocean with salty crisp breezes and blue-gray sea curving into a forever horizon. We even had background music to add to the romantic ambience. And except for the "can't kiss because he's my brother" thing, this was the perfect romantic moment.

But any minute Grammy would whisk my soul away with no warning. Then good-bye beach and spring break. Zap! Back into a hospital bed and my own body.

But shouldn't I have a choice about when and where my soul traveled?

Admittedly, I'd made some mistakes as a Temp Lifer, but I'd tried hard. I'd even helped take down a Dark Lifer. If I could take out a Dark Lifer (or at least point to where he was), why shouldn't I be allowed to finish my assignment?

Not being the type of girl to stand by when I could be taking action, I came to a drastic decision.

Eli was staring at gyrating bodies on the beach when I tapped his shoulder. I gestured that I was going to get something to drink from a nearby snack cart. "I'll be right back," I said.

"I'll wait here," he promised, then returned to watching the dancing.

I bought a drink (non-alcoholic, thank you very much) from the snack cart. Sipping water, I glanced around to make sure no one was watching. Then I withdrew the GEM from my pocket.

I bent down low, opening it to the first page, and whispered, "GEM, can you get a message to Grammy Greta?"

A bold *YES* flourished across the page.

"I thought so. Please tell her that we need to talk."

As I stared at the book, the page burst into video of Grammy's gentle, smiling face. Instead of words flashing, I felt a pressure in my ears as if someone had stuck in an ear bud, and I clearly heard Grammy.

"Hi, honey." It was mind-boggling how I could read her lips on the GEM page at the same time she broadcast into my ears.

"Grammy! It's so good to hear you!" I whispered, tears coming to my eyes because, no matter how many times I'd seen her since her death, she was dead and I missed her.

"I heard you spotted the Dark Lifer. Great work," she said proudly.

"You really mean that? Even after I messed up by losing the GEM and having no clue how to act like Sharayah?"

"You've done fine and I'm the one who owes you an apology for putting you in such a challenging situation without any training. I admit to acting on impulse when I discovered you knew Sharayah's brother. At the time, this seemed like a simple assignment, but I didn't know about the Dark Lifer. I'm really sorry."

"Don't be. This has been a great assignment, and except for the scary stuff, it's been fun. I figured out a lot of things about Sharayah and even got my GEM back—Eli drove four hundred miles to bring it to me. I think you'd really like him, Grammy."

"I already do," she said with a knowing lift of her brows. "He's a very nice boy—and I have it on good authority that you'll be seeing a lot of him."

"You do?" I felt my cheeks get sizzling hot.

"Some future events are written in the Hall of Records and I've been known to sneak a peak when it concerns people I love. So I know you have many wonderful things ahead of you once you're in your right body—which is what brings me here. You have good timing, contacting me just as I was preparing to contact you."

"You were?" I gulped, tempted to slam the book shut and run away.

"It's time, Amber. Your parents will be so happy when you wake up."

I thought of Mom and Dad and what I'd already put them through. It was selfish of me to resist going back, yet that's what I felt inside. Maybe my resistance was a leftover from Sharayah's soul, some sort of defense system holding tightly to me like someone drowning grabs onto a life jacket. I was Sharayah's life jacket.

"Grammy, there's something I have to tell you," I said, drawing a deep breath. "About my assignment."

"What, honey?"

"As much as I want to return to my own life, I can't leave yet. I need to finish my assignment. I know how to solve Sharayah's problems."

"Temp Lifers are replacements, not guardian angels."

"Can't I be both?"

"Oh, Amber, you make me so proud." Her tone embraced me, loving and warm, but the smile she gave seemed a little sad. "Unfortunately, there is little you can do for Sharayah. She has to live her own life."

"But I can make her life happier if I have more time. And the reason you were pulling me back today was because of the

Dark Lifer, only the DD Team took care of Warren so there's no danger."

"Danger wears many faces," she said.

"Don't worry about me, Grammy. I'll be fine, but I'm not so sure about Sharayah. I'm afraid she won't go to the audition unless I'm her."

"I suspect you're right."

"So you see why I can't change back yet? Grammy, give me—give Sharayah—another chance."

"It's not that simple," she argued, but with less fervor.

"Only twenty-four hours. Then I'll happily switch back."

"You have no idea what you're asking."

"Grammy, let me do this. It's important for Sharayah . . . and me, too."

"Well . . . " Her voice wavered.

"Please," I said quietly.

Clouds rose white and misty around my grandmother's face as she gave a slow nod. "Well . . . all right. One more day—and not a minute more."

I thought I heard my grandmother sigh.

Then the GEM slammed itself shut.

Eli and I celebrated my "one more day" by indulging in chocolate.

We wandered down streets until we found a shop called *Choco Lots!* The Amber inside me drooled with passion. Choosing just one candy was impossible, so Eli and I systemically divided the candies into categories and mathematically selected a representation of each chocolate category to share. When I started to offer my "borrowed" credit card, Eli shook his head and paid in cash.

"You are the best brother ever," I said as we left the store with two bags.

"I don't feel at all brotherly with you. But then I look at you and see my sister. Like this scar on your arm." He pointed to a small white line below my elbow. "I bet you don't know how that happened."

I shook my head. "No idea."

"But I do. I was six, and you were teaching me how to ride my bike."

"I was a nice sister," I observed, moving aside with Eli to make room for a couple with a stroller.

"You were the best," he agreed a bit sadly. "It was when Dad was starting his dealership and Mom did his bookkeeping, leaving us with babysitters a lot. It was Sharayah who put me up on a bike, explained what to do and pushed me into the street. But a car turned onto our street and was headed for me. Sharayah ran after me, grabbed the bike and threw us out of the way. I fell on the grass, but she had to go to the emergency room for stitches. That's the Sharayah I miss."

"She's around, just in hiding," I said. "She'll come back."

"I hope so."

"Until then, you've got me."

"Yeah," he said, smiling. "I like that."

"You know what I like?"

"What?" He gave me a look that was far from brotherly.

"What else?" I reached into the bag and we shared a chocolate-covered strawberry.

That afternoon will probably go down as the most romantic platonic non date in history. No kissing, hand holding or body contact of any kind. We walked along the beach without even brushing fingertips. We found a small amusement park and rode on fast rides, sitting a safe "sibling distance" apart. Despite all this non-touching, I felt closer to Eli than ever.

After a late lunch of chili hot dogs and onion rings, I was

staring at a spot of chili on his mouth, wishing I could kiss it off, when Eli glanced at the clock on his cell phone and said he had to leave. Turns out he wasn't lying about having friends to visit. He invited me to go along, but keeping up the Big Sister pretense privately was hard enough; it would be insane around people who actually knew Sharayah.

So I wandered back to the beach.

Mauve was exactly where I'd left her, sitting on the towel with her elbows on her knees. She was leaning her head against her hands in a wistful way, watching a guy around thirty and a toddler girl about the age of my triplet sisters. The guy, who was probably the father, was showing the little girl how to dig in the sand with a plastic shovel. Mauve was so absorbed in watching that she didn't notice me until I plopped down on the hot sand beside her. When she lifted her face, I was stunned to see tears streaming down her cheeks.

"Mauve, what's wrong?" I asked in concern. "Why are you crying?"

She wiped her eyes. "I'm not. Just something in my eye."

"Yeah—tears."

"Forget it," she said sharply. "I'm fine."

"No, you aren't. Did something happen with Alonzo?"

"No. We're cool."

"So why are you crying alone on the beach? And you had the oddest expression while you watched them." I pointed as the little girl giggled when her father shoveled sand over her toes. "Do you know them?"

"No." She sounded angry now. "And stop acting like you don't know what's going on. We talked about this when you saw the picture. I appreciate your support, but I warned you never to bring it up again. You're just trying to get me to talk about it, and I already told you I'm not going to."

Hmmm, this was getting interesting. Unfortunately, I hadn't seen any picture so I had no clue what was going on.

"I read this book once, called *Talk Therapy,* that said how it was healthy to talk about problems. You can hide them from others but not from yourself—that was some of the advice."

"Self-help books suck. And since when do you read books that don't have half-naked men on the cover?" She brushed sand off her towel, turning her back on me. "Go away, Rayah. Hang out with your brother if you're bored."

"Eli is visiting his friends."

"So find Sadie. She'll talk about anything."

"Except for the problems she's trying to hide," I said.

"Don't compare me with her," Mauve warned. "My issues aren't anything like Sadie's. I'm not a klepto."

"You know about her stealing?" I blew out a heavy sigh.

"Hel-lo? I'm the one who warned you Sadie had stolen your ATM card and that you better switch all your money to another bank."

I thought of the cash in my purse, finally understanding. Sharayah wasn't carrying all that cash for any nefarious reasons. She meant to put it into a new account in a different bank—only I'd interrupted by taking over her body.

"—and never leave your purse around when Sadie comes to our room," Mauve added. "She can't help herself if she sees jewelry, credit cards or cash. She's my friend and all, but she's a thief. At least she's been better since she got arrested—"

"Arrested!" My hand flew to my mouth and I tasted sand. Yuck.

"Shhsh! Not so loud," Mauve cautioned, looking around nervously. "We promised not to tell anyone as long as Sadie continues with her therapy. But she's missing her session this week, so I'm worried about a relapse. We have to watch her carefully. Have you seen her take anything?"

I nodded. "A rhinestone watch."

"Damn." Mauve scowled. "When did this happen?"

"Yesterday."

"And you're just now telling me?" Mauve gave me a disgusted look. "You promised to let me know right away so I could prevent anything serious from happening."

I stared at her, marveling at this new side of Mauve. It was almost like she had a heart. "You really do care about Sadie, don't you?"

"She's my friend." Mauve shrugged. "And you are, too, even though you can be a total bitch sometimes."

"Me?" I gasped.

"You never talk about your past, but sometimes it's like you're on self-destruct. I can't always be there to pick up the pieces—although I try. You have to be responsible. Guys are fun, but they don't stick around when you need them."

"Not all guys," I pointed out. "Eli ... I mean, my brother, is the loyal type."

"Your brother's too young for me," she said wryly.

But not for me, I thought.

"What about Alonzo?" I asked Mauve, trying to understand. "Things seem to be progressing nicely with him."

"When spring break is over, so are we—if we last that long. He was pissed when I didn't want to dance, so he's probably already gone on to some other girl. I know better than to expect anything from him. We girls have to watch each others' backs—guys just want to have fun with no responsibilities."

Her tone hinted at a betrayal so deep an X-ray would probably show scaring across her heart. And when her gaze strayed back to the father and daughter, I wondered if she had issues with her own father. Except it wasn't the man she was staring at—it was the little girl. A suspicion came to me. But I couldn't just come out and ask her something so personal— especially something I was supposed to already know. How was I going to find out?

"That little girl is cute," I said carefully. "She's about the age of my...um...the little triplet sisters of this girl I know."

"Triplets! I can't imagine carrying three babies at once. The mother must have horrible stretch marks."

"She had a C-section, and was on bed rest for months."

"What a nightmare. I'd never want to go through that."

And just the way she said it, I knew her secret without Grammy, Sharayah or even the GEM telling me.

"Mauve, can you show me the picture again?" I asked softly. "Of your daughter."

*

You never really know people, even when they stay in their own body.

Mauve had seemed all bitchy and irresponsible, but that was only the outside. Inside, she loved so much that when a guy broke her heart and left her pregnant, she gave up the baby to an adoptive family who needed to give love as much as the baby needed to be loved.

When Mauve showed me the picture of herself holding a baby, I could have cried. The baby was two years old now and named Jenna, and Mauve's only contact was a picture in the mail every year on Jenna's birthday. In a private way, Mauve was a genuine heroine and I respected her, maybe even liked her. I had less respect for Sadie—who'd seemed so fun and nice when we'd first met, but couldn't be trusted.

For the first time since living in a college-aged body, my soul caught up in experience. I felt even older than Sharayah. Things that seemed important a week ago—making welcome baskets to give to new students at school, achieving a 4.0 average and trying not to show how uncool I really was despite all the self-help books—seemed unimportant. When I was me again, I'd look the same, but inside I'd be forever changed.

My emotions were still raw a few hours later, when Sadie, Mauve and I met up at the crappo condo. None of us had planned to meet, but here we all were. Together again, pretending that nothing had changed.

"I'm so over Warren," Sadie insisted as she rifled through her suitcase until she found a jade-green tube dress. "Let's have a girls' night out at Club Revolution."

"I'm in," Mauve said as she tried to figure out the latch on the fold-out bed. "And I'm going to wear my sexiest dress tonight so that when Alonzo sees me, he'll regret going off with that tramp in the pink bikini."

"At least Alonzo isn't in jail," Sadie said sadly.

"Better him than you," Mauve said with a meaningful look. "Did you take care of things?"

"I don't know what you're talking about," Sadie retorted, all wide-eyed and innocent.

"You know exactly what I mean." Mauve narrowed her eyes. "Did you?"

"What do you think? That I'm stupid? I'll handle it when I'm ready, okay?" Sadie glared back at Mauve, then slammed her suitcase. "I'm going to shower."

She stormed off, the door banging so loud behind her that I jumped.

"That went well," Mauve said with a grim smile.

"You think?" I shook my head, sure they were both insane.

"Actually, yes. By tonight she'll forget about hating me and tell me about whatever new guy she's interested in. It's not like she needs to steal—her parents are both lawyers and loaded. She just does it for attention, so I give her attention and she's okay. Some problems are easy to fix."

Mauve said this so sadly, I knew she was thinking about her daughter again.

But there would be no more talking about this or any other problems tonight.

It was Girls' Night Out—and we were going to party.

✳

Club Revolution was tucked behind a church and a liquor store, almost hidden beyond the crush of bodies flowing into it. By the time we arrived, the place was rocking with wild music. People weren't just dancing inside the club, either, but outside on the terrace, hands waving and laughter rippling like uncorked champagne.

Walking between my two roommates, I felt self-conscious,

wondering if everyone was comparing us. Gorgeous, pink-haired Mauve wore a slinky halter-top with black leather pants; petite Sadie had her long braids coiled high on her head and held in place with a glittery tiara that made her look like an exotic princess; and tall, thin Sharayah, excited but nervous, wore a long-sleeved, white knit shirt over a swirled skirt—which was a little boring for clubbing, but had a hidden pocket which was perfect for tucking away the GEM.

My last night as Sharayah, I thought, with both relief and regret. I planned to have fun—but within reason. Which is why when my friends offered to get me a drink, I said I'd go get my own, and bought a Coke. (Rum and Coke, I'd tell anyone who asked.)

We made our way to a table, sitting down with our drinks. Immediately a blond guy with wire-rimmed glasses came over and asked Mauve to dance. She checked him out, smiled as if she liked what she saw, then drained her drink in one gulp and waved at us as she headed for the dance floor.

Sadie watched her enviously and said something to me, but the band was so loud I couldn't hear her. She gestured to me and then to the dancing crowd, tilting her head in a *You want to dance?* gesture.

I shook my head and mouthed, "No."

Sadie shrugged, then went off on her own, melting into the throng of dancers.

The music was so fantastic, like an invisible magnet pulling at my body. Maybe I would join Sadie. It wasn't like I needed a guy to dance with. Girls danced together all the time. Or I could just sit here, sip my drink and think "strategy" for the *Voice Choice* competition.

Eli had agreed to drive me, and we were leaving before daylight. I didn't expect the competition to be huge like the mega-thousands lining up for *American Idol*—there would probably be only a few hundred entrants. Still, I had to make sure Sharayah got noticed. Luckily I'd read lots of books about the music industry and knew that gimmicks like showing up in a costume were for amateurs. Professionalism and perfect pitch were key. Sharayah already had a great voice; I'd supply the professional attitude.

Song selection would be tricky. I had a few ideas, but wasn't sure which suited Sharayah's voice best. Eli could help me decide, I thought, taking another sip of Coke.

It seemed like fate was paving the way for Sharayah's singing stardom. She had the voice, I had the know-how and Eli would be there for support.

What could go wrong?

As if thinking about Eli had its own magical power, I looked up and there he was.

"So how'd you get in? Aren't you underage?" I teased.

"No younger than you," he said, loud enough to be overheard even in the noisy nightclub.

"But my I.D. shows I'm twenty-one."

"I.D. isn't so hard to come by ... one way or another." His smile always curved a little unevenly, which was so cute. He was dressed in black slacks and a button-down beige shirt—probably too formal for a beach-themed nightclub where half the dancers wore swim trunks or bikinis, but I thought he looked perfect.

I gestured for him to sit down, but he shook his head and pointed to the dance floor. "Want to dance?"

My feet were tapping and my body swaying, so the answer was yes. I did want to dance, and specifically with him. I stood and clasped his hand; his gentle yet firm, warm, comfortable hand that I wanted to hold forever.

As we neared the dancers, a familiar pink-haired girl slipped out of the crowd and hurried toward us.

"I see you changed your mind about dancing." Although the sound was louder on the dance floor, the acoustics must have been better because I could hear Mauve fine.

I nodded. "Yeah. Eli asked me."

"You're going to dance with *him?*" she asked incredulously.

Eli and I immediately dropped our hands and stepped apart.

Mauve rolled her eyes, then looked closer at Eli. "Too young, but cute enough for some fun. Go find someone who doesn't share your DNA, Rayah, and I'll dance with little bro."

Then she grabbed Eli's hand and jerked him toward her. Eli shot me a helpless *what can I do?* look before he was swallowed by the crowd and I lost sight of him. Embarrassed, I stood there—not sure whether to retreat back to the table or join the dancers.

After sitting alone for what felt like hours, but was probably only fifteen minutes, I felt someone tap my shoulder.

"Guess who," a deep voice whispered in my ear.

I'd only heard him once before, but with my shoulder tingling from the gentle touch, I knew exactly who stood behind me.

Slowly, I turned around.

Dyce wore his cap slightly tilted to one side, along with dark blue slacks, a gray windbreaker and a satisfied smile. "I didn't expect to see you again."

"Me either," I told him. "But I hope you aren't planning to ask me to dance. I was in the mood, but that's over and gone now."

"Who wants to dance at a dance club?"

"You're teasing me," I protested, blushing. "And it's not that I don't like dancing. I do, a lot, it's just that..." *Babbling Alert* flashed in my head and I stopped before I completely lost all my pride. "Anyway, what brings you here?"

"I came with some friends, but they've ditched me and I'm getting tired of waiting around for them."

I frowned at the writhing dance floor. "I know what you mean."

"You've been ditched, too?" he guessed.

"Not exactly. Everyone else just wanted to dance."

"Except you," he guessed with a sympathetic nod. "This band is all noise and no substance. I can't stand another minute in here. Come on, let's go outside."

I didn't agree with Dyce about the band—the music was rockin' with a raunchy edge that almost lifted me out of my chair. I peered through swaying bodies, searching for Eli or my friends, but a spinning strobe light distorted colors and shapes, making my eyes ache. I wanted to dance—but only with Eli. Although he hadn't intentionally left me, it bothered me that he'd gone along with Mauve, who thought he was cute. And why hadn't they come back yet? The band was on a new song, yet there was no sign of Sadie, Mauve or Eli returning for me and I wasn't about to dive into that crowd searching for them. I was done waiting around—they could just come and find me.

I followed Dyce past the bar and its cushioned stools, through a door and then outside. Clouds blew fiercely, chilling my bones and making me almost turn around and run back into the warmth. But as if reading my mind, Dyce took off his windbreaker and wrapped it around me.

"Better?" he asked.

"Yeah. Thanks." That feeling I'd noticed yesterday, a deep hot stirring inside, rippled through me. "Um ... this wasn't a good idea. I should go back in."

"Why? Will your friends miss you?"

"Eventually."

"Until they do, stay and talk with me."

"Well ... for a few minutes. You did save my life yesterday."

"I was lucky to be nearby at the right time. Anyone would have done the same thing."

"Not just anyone," I pointed out. "You were really brave."

"And you're really beautiful tonight," he said, in such a sincere way that I forgot how to breathe for a second.

"Um ... I just feel cold." I rubbed my hands together.

"If you're too cold, we can go inside."

I glanced back, unable to see more than reflections and light through the tinted windows. The raucous music seemed to rock the building and the buzz of voices—shouts, laughter, squeals spilled through the air. Sharayah would never have left; she'd be dancing like a force of nature until she dropped. That's what I should have done, too. But I just couldn't work up the energy. Standing outside, under clouds that shifted to allow glimpses of a half-moon, with wind tousling my hair and tasting of salty surf, both bitter and sweet, I felt content. Underneath my party dress and makeup, I was still me. And I'd always loved quiet moments alone with nature.

But I was far from alone—Dyce was leaning close, studying my face as if it were a map.

I shrugged. "I'll stay outside for a while."

"Then you should move around, get your blood flowing so you don't freeze." He pointed beyond the parking lot to where night lamps twinkled over roofs and pavement. "Let's walk on the path."

I followed his gaze to a graveled path leading toward the marina; high masts and sails swayed in the distance like pale ghosts. Walking was the least offensive type of exercise, so I followed him.

We went along the path for a short way until we stepped up onto a wooden dock. It swayed slightly with the undulating breath of the sea, waves slamming against the wood and spitting spray.

"Beautiful, isn't it?" Dyce said, leaning against a rail and staring off into the night-ocean.

Standing beside him, I stared off too, and nodded. Beautiful hardly began to describe the glinting half-moon's glow on the silvery waves. I wrapped his jacket around me tighter, inhaling salty sea and a whiff of something I could only define as "Dyce": musky, spicy, and mysterious.

"This night reminds of me of Robert Browning's famous lines," he said. "*And the yellow half-moon large and low; And the startled little waves that leap, In fiery ringlets from their sleep.*" He turned to peer down into my face. "I sense something in you, Sharayah, some sort of fire. Tell me about yourself."

"What's to tell? I'm here for spring break, just like a thousand other girls."

"But you're different than other girls."

"That can be good and bad." Okay, I was flirting a little, but it was harmless because he had a girlfriend and I (hopefully) had a boyfriend.

"From my view, it's all good. You have a poet's soul," he said.

"Me? I can't recite any poems, except a silly one about a fuzzy bear." I laughed, taking all his flowery talk like a game. I mean, really! What normal guy talked like this? It was like he was a throwback to the Renaissance era. Still, I have enough of an ego that I loved the flattery.

"I can teach you poems and much more," he said huskily.

"Whoa," I said with a firm shake of my head. "This has been fun and all, but we both know it's not going anywhere. I have a guy I like and you already have a girlfriend."

"I do?" He arched his brows in a question.

"Come on, Dyce, you told me how you couldn't wait to get back to her yesterday. Your girlfriend—Emmy."

"Oh … Emmy." The confusion on his face spread into a dazzling smile. "Right, she's amazing and I can't wait to get back to her."

"That's what I guessed. She's probably waiting for you right now, so you should go."

"I will, and you should, too. Come with me. I want you to meet her."

"You can't be serious."

"But I am." He reached for my hand, and while I knew I should resist, I didn't. Our fingers touched with such a delicious tingle that I almost forgot how to think.

"I-I can't." It took all my energy to pull back my hand, and when I did, the sweet warmth faded away to a numb chill. "I really can't. I've already been gone too long," I added trying to convince myself. I glanced up the hill to the bright lights of the dance club.

"But it'll only take a few minutes. Emmy is just over there." He pointed toward the marina. "You'll love her as much as I do."

"I guarantee you—your girlfriend won't love meeting

me." Guys could be so dense sometimes…yet it was kind of sweet. "Now I really have to get back to my friends."

"Five minutes, that's all it will take," he persisted.

There was something so vulnerable and sincere about him that I hesitated, touched by how much he loved his girlfriend. And I owed him a lot after rescuing me yesterday. If this was all he wanted in return, how could I refuse?

So with a sigh, I nodded.

I followed him down a graveled path, around a boat repair yard and down steep steps to the marina. We passed sailboats and two huge yachts, then stopped abruptly at a mid-sized boat. Dyce pointed proudly. "Here she is."

Under the yellowy light from a nearby lamp, I looked around for a girl but only saw boats. And then I noticed the name of the boat we faced: Emmeline.

"Emmy," I said, finally getting it.

"She's my girl," he told me. "And my home."

"You live here?" I asked, surprised because the boat didn't look bigger than thirty feet, or deep enough to have more than a cramped room below the deck.

"Temporarily," he answered. "I don't sleep well on land, perhaps because I come from a long line of seaman and have saltwater in my blood. Although this isn't actually my boat. It's a rental, but she's still a beaut. A 1991 Bayliner Cierra Sunbridge—fully equipped galley with stove, fridge, sink, shower, digital depth sounder, pinion power steering, and AM/FM stereo with four built-in speakers."

I nodded appreciatively, although I only understood part of what he said.

"So come aboard and I'll give you a tour," he invited me,

with such a sexy, intriguing smile that I was sorely tempted—which is exactly why I refused.

"Can't," I told him. "My friends will worry if I don't return soon."

"It won't take long. And I think you'll be interested in some special things I have—a poetry book that belonged to my great-great-grandfather and dates back to the mid-1800s."

"Wow—that's old."

"Leather binding and signed by the author. It's a work of art."

"Is it safe to travel with such a valuable book? Shouldn't it be under glass?"

"Books are meant to be read, not hidden. Besides, I keep it in an airtight trunk, along with several others." He cocked his head, watching me expectantly.

"No. This all sounds interesting, but I have to go now. Thanks for the rescue and everything."

"Come on, Sharayah," he said in a tone as lulling as a gentle surf.

"I've already stayed longer than I should."

As I stepped back, he pointed behind me. "Wait!" he shouted. "Watch where you're—"

It all happened so fast. I wasn't sure how my feet got tangled in the thick coil of rope, but I felt my spiked heel snagging, then my arms flailing and Dyce lunging for me. As I fell backward, my shoulder slammed into a gate leading down to a dock bordering the ocean, cracking the hinges with a sharp metallic sound. Crying out from the pain, I tried to steady myself but couldn't grab hold of anything solid, and I careened backwards...

"Sharayah! Take my arm!"

Dyce grabbed for me, only he seemed to lose his balance, too, and next thing I knew I was falling through an opening where there used to be a gate. Screaming, I tumbled and fell...

Into the ocean.

Stabbed by needles of icy water, I went down, down, shocked beyond thought. Salt water filled my mouth and pain ripped through me. I couldn't breathe or think; the world blurred with freezing horror. Panic exploded; my own screams were drowning in my head. A voice somewhere inside me shouted *Kick! Swim! Fight!*

But my arms were heavy weights wrapped in fabric and my shoes anchors dragging me down. Gagging on salt water. Can't breathe, need air, sinking... until something splashed next to me and strong hands pulled me, lifted me, and I gulped air.

"Don't struggle," Dyce's words swam in my head.

I hadn't realized I was struggling, and stopped. Then I was literally carried away in his arms. My teeth clattered with cold. I couldn't stop shivering. Coughing, gasping, spitting salt water. Then the chill eased as we went down a staircase, out of the biting wind, and onto a boat. Emmeline, I realized.

Dyce bent slightly, opened a door, and carried me down a folding staircase into a dark but cozy and warm cabin. Then he gently lowered me onto a cushioned bench. There was a click as he turned on a wall switch and light flooded the room.

"Are you okay?" he asked, leaning over me. "I'm so sorry

that happened—I tried to warn you about the rope but you fell too fast and I couldn't stop you. Damned rope. Can I get anything for you?"

"Sooo cold," I chattered through clenched teeth.

"Right." In two steps, he crossed the compact room to a built-in cabinet and opened a drawer. He tossed me a striped blue towel. "Here."

I caught the towel. "Thanks."

Taking off the jacket he'd loaned me, I rubbed the towel over my soggy blouse and skirt, noticing with some embarrassment the dripping wet puddle I made on his bench cushions.

"S-sorry, I-I'm getting your boat all ... all wet," I shivered.

"That doesn't matter, but you do, and you'll catch pneumonia if you don't put on warm clothes."

"I-I don't have anything else—and only one shoe." I pointed to the single black spiked shoe. The other must have been still stuck in the rope or sunk to the bottom of the sea.

"Fortunately, I keep spare clothes in my cubby up top. I'll be back in a minute." He climbed up the steps and pushed through the narrow doorway.

I worked the towel over my clothes but when drops of stinging sea water kept dribbling in my eyes, I wrapped the towel turban-style around my hair.

Then I sank back on the cushioned bench, exhausted but grateful to Dyce. That made it twice he'd rescued me, like he was a superhero in disguise. I wouldn't have drowned—I can swim—but I'd been so shocked by the cold sea and so weighed down with clothes that I'd panicked. I was lucky that one shoe was the only casualty.

Or was it?

What about my GEM?

"No!" I cried, remembering the time I'd been soaking in a bubble bath and dropped a book into the tub. The book had swelled up with water, the pages sticking together, then warping, even after I dried it with a blow dryer.

I jumped up so suddenly that my towel turban raveled to the floor. I reached into my skirt pocket and pulled out a completely dry book.

Amazed, I quickly opened the GEM and the familiar blank pages rustled with a soft flutter that seemed to chastise me for doubting their magic. A drop of sea water slid down my soggy hair and plopped onto the pristine paper, blotting only for a second and then fading until the page shone like new. My chill was fading, too, now that I was out of the cold night and warming in the cozy cabin.

Staring down at the small book, I thought of everything I'd been through in the last two days. Many things were still unresolved and I could really use some answers, but it was hard to know what to ask my GEM first:

- What happened to Warren after his capture?
- Will Sharayah win the *Voice Choice* contest?
- Will Alyce forgive me for not returning today?
- Has Eli noticed I'm gone or is he still dancing?

Torn between the practical questions I should ask and the emotional ones my heart longed to know, I started with the first question.

"What happened to Warren?" I whispered into the GEM.

He returned to his dwelling.

Huh? What did that mean? Maybe the book misunderstood and thought I wanted to know what happened to the innocent victim who owned Warren's body. So I rephrased my question, this time specifying that I wanted to know what happened to the Dark Lifer posing as Warren.

Unable to locate the Dark Lifer.

Okay, now I was really confused. I'd watched the DD Team capture Warren yet the book was saying they couldn't "locate" the Dark Lifer. Had he escaped from them? I opened my mouth to ask this when I froze. Footsteps approaching!

Quickly, I shoved the GEM back inside my pocket.

"Here you go!" Dyce called from the hatch-like door at the top of the stairs as he tossed down clothes. "Holler up when you're dressed and I'll come back."

The door shut behind him with a soft bang, and I was grateful for the clothes—as well as Dyce's gentlemanly behavior. Most guys would have stuck around, waiting for a free show. But Dyce wasn't like most guys.

Hastily, I stripped out of my clothes and folded them in a pile on the oblong table that was sticking up like a flat umbrella on a metal pole. Then I reached for the clothes, expecting baggy uncomfortable men's clothes but pleasantly surprised to find a pink scooped-necked blouse, skinny denim jeans, a lacy bra and red satin bikini underwear ... all in a perfect size for Sharayah.

Whoa! Why did a bachelor have girl's clothes conveniently on his rental boat? Did all rental boats come equipped with assorted spare clothing? Or was this a freaky coincidence... not that I believed in coincidences. In my experience, things usually happened either for a good reason or for a suspicious one. And my intuition strongly hinted at the latter option.

Then I noticed something which added to this puzzle—a price tag dangling from the jeans. I whistled at the price—an amount that would have taken me six months to earn babysitting. Why did Dyce have expensive women's clothing? Had he lied about having a girlfriend?

I was trying to figure out a tactful way to ask this when he returned with food. My Amber appetite rose up like a feral beast, sniffing delicious smells and ready to pounce on the fresh strawberries, cheese and vanilla wafers. But I resisted the "scarf" impulse and politely thanked him. He also had a porcelain cup of warm tea on his tray, which had a sweet yet tart aroma.

As he set down the tray, I noticed a discolored gash on his lower arm that hadn't been there before he'd pulled me out of the water. Instantly, guilt washed over me. I hadn't even asked how he was after he jumped in to rescue me. He'd brought me clothes but hadn't taken the time to change out of his own dripping clothes. He probably was miserable, yet all he seemed concerned about was me. I was a selfish, ungrateful klutz.

So I immediately and sincerely said, "Thank you. I really mean it."

"No problem." He set the tray on a small table. "Hope you like the food. It's all I could find."

I sniffed the tea, detecting almond and spices. "Smells yummy."

"Do you recognize the flavor?"

"No," I said, "but it's very nice. What is it?"

"Almond spice black tea." He pursed his lips together as if bothered by something. "Are you sure you've never had it before?"

"Never, but I'm enjoying it now." I took a sip, warmed by the heat and intrigued by the nutty, bitter taste. "Thanks for hot tea and dry clothes. I was wondering about the clothes ... they look new. How did you happen to have them?"

He shrugged. "I bought them for someone special."

"So you do have a girlfriend?" I took another sip.

"Not any more."

"Oh ... sorry it didn't work out."

"Disappointments are learning experiences," he said. "I'm wiser and won't make that mistake again."

There was a subtle anger in his tone that made me uneasy. I set the tea cup down and stood abruptly. "I really have to go now. Leave me your address and I'll mail the clothes back to you."

"Keep them." He pointed to the plate, which I hadn't touched. "At least eat something before you go."

"I'm not that hungry."

"But they're your favorites."

"Excuse me?" I stopped short, staring at him. "How would you know?"

"You mentioned it earlier."

"No, I'm sure I didn't." My uneasiness intensified and I realized how vulnerable I was, in a boat with a strange guy. No one even knew where I was. "I need to leave now."

He blocked my way to the ladder. "Enjoy your tea. I know

it's your favorite, just like I know about the wafers and strawberries. And you should recognize the clothes, too."

"What are you talking about?"

"Haven't you figured it out yet? I've been waiting a long time to be with you." Dyce rubbed his stubbly chin. "We have so much to talk about."

"We never met before yesterday. I don't know you."

"But I know all about you."

"You have me mixed up with someone else."

"No," he said simply, with a confident, creepy smile.

But what creeped me out even more than his smile was a jolting realization.

Dyce was right about the clothes—I did recognize the pink blouse and the skinny jeans. I'd never worn them, but this body had. They were identical to what Sharayah had been wearing when I'd dreamed about her climbing on the ocean bluff, when her romantic hopes were crushed by Gabe's cruelty.

"Gauguin said it best," Dyce told me with eerie calm. *"Life being what it is, one dreams of revenge."* Then he reached for a roll of duct tape.

D uct tape!
That's what Gabe used on Sharayah!

Totally freaked out, I backed up on the bench, desperate to get out of there. But there was nowhere to go. The wood-paneled room only had tiny portholes for windows, and no doors except the small hatch at the top of the steps.

And Dyce blocked the steps.

"What's this about?" I cried, looking around for something to defend myself but seeing nothing within reach except cushions.

"We have a mutual friend." His tone, accusing and angry, and the way he twirled the roll of duct tape around his finger, told me more than his words.

"Do you mean … Gabe?"

"And the pretty lady wins a prize." He chuckled darkly. "Hold out your hands."

"Been there, done that. I'm not falling for that again." I threw my hands behind my back. "Just let me out of here."

"After I went to so much trouble to get you here? I don't think so."

Shock zapped through me. "You planned this?"

"Yes, although you didn't act as I expected so I had to improvise."

"Improvise?" I exclaimed furiously. "You knocked me in the water on purpose?"

"Nothing I do is by accident."

"Why would you let me fall into the water, then jump in and pull me out?"

"To get you onto my boat and finish what was started months ago."

"But we only met yesterday. I don't understand what you want from me."

"I don't expect you to. I've been preparing for months," he confessed with a self-satisfied expression. "I studied you methodically: learning poetry from your favorite authors, filling the pantry with your favorite foods and drinks. I know your worst secrets."

There was something familiar about his words.

"The threats!" I choked out. "You sent them, too?"

"I might have." He moved closer with the roll of duct tape.

"Then the redhead wasn't my stalker—it was you!"

"What redhead?"

"A girl from my school, but that doesn't matter now. Just

let me go, and I won't press any charges against you or tell anyone about this. I'll pretend it never happened."

"But I want you to remember. The threats were to remind you about what you've done. Don't play dumb. You know what I'm talking about."

Yes, I did. But only because I'd relived Sharayah's memory of what happened last winter on the stormy cliff. Even now, I trembled at the memory of Gabe falling and lying motionless on the jagged rocks.

"I know what happened," Dyce said, glaring. "Gabe told me."

"Impossible! How could he when he's—"

"Dead? Sorry to disappoint you, but he survived."

"I'm not disappointed, I'm thrilled!" I sagged in relief. "That's great news! I'm so glad he's alive."

"No thanks to you," Dyce spat out. "You left him and ran away."

"I went to get a rope or find someone to help."

"Sure you did," he scoffed.

"I did! But when I got back, Gabe wasn't there. And the tide had come in so I thought he'd drowned."

"Yet you did nothing about it."

"What could I do? I tried to report it but no one believed me."

"You wanted him dead."

I shook my head, remembering Sharayah's overwhelming love for Gabe, how she trusted him even when he called her a fool and turned violent. If he hadn't fallen, he would have done something horrible, I was sure of it, and I was glad he'd fallen. But that's not what Sharayah felt. I didn't need to consult the

GEM to know her whole transformation into a bad girl was a reaction to grief. An important part of her had died when he fell. And now this jerk was trying to make things worse. Well, he was dealing with the wrong Sharayah. I may not know much about college life, but I knew about survival and wasn't afraid to fight for what I wanted.

"If Gabe is alive, why didn't he tell anyone?" I demanded. "Where has he been all this time?"

"Do you really care?" he asked skeptically.

"I shouldn't—not after what he did." My fear surged into anger. "You accuse me of trying to hurt Gabe, when he was the one who attacked me. Do you know what he did that night?"

Dyce eyed me warily and nodded.

"Of course you do or you wouldn't be waving that duct tape. What did he tell you? A lie about how I pushed him over the cliff? The only reason he fell was because he pulled this Jekyll and Hyde attitude and attacked me. When we struggled, he fell and I couldn't help him with my hands taped."

"You left him bleeding and suffering."

"That's not fair! What he did was worse—killing the hope and trust of a girl who loved him. Whatever sick revenge you have planned can't hurt worse than thinking the man you love more than life is dead."

"Are you sure about that?" He gave me a look that shot chills through my already shivering skin.

I swallowed hard, glancing at the stairs and contemplating the odds of success if I made a run for it. I had less than a five percent chance of getting past him before he'd grab me. No one knew I was here, so a rescue from my "rescuer" was out of the question. My only option was to convince him to let me go.

"Dyce, why are you really doing this?" I asked.

He spun the duct tape in deliberate circles as he leaned closer to me. "Gabe had plans that night which he wasn't able to finish. So I'll do it for him."

"I don't believe Gabe would want you to hurt someone he loved."

"You never really knew him."

"But you do?" I scoffed.

He nodded. "Like we're the same person."

"And he approves of this?" I asked with disgust, gesturing around the room that now felt like a prison. "Revenge on me won't help him."

"There are different degrees of revenge, and honor has merit, too, although I don't expect you to understand." He spoke in a harsh formal tone that was different from how he'd spoken when we first met. His mannerisms had altered in subtle yet decisive ways; he spoke less like a teen and more like someone older even than my parents.

"You're right—I don't understand." I forced myself to remain calm. The most important lesson I'd learned from all my self help books was to stay confident and never admit weakness. No fear was allowed in kidnappings and the music biz. "If Gabe is okay, why did he send you instead of coming himself?"

"He can't move in his body."

"Paralyzed? So he's like in a wheelchair? Ohmygod!" I whispered hoarsely. "That's horrible. Why didn't he tell me? I would have helped."

"Like you helped him over the cliff?"

"That was an accident, and I was horrified when it happened. I'm sorry he's hurt, but none of this will heal him. Don't you realize that kidnapping is serious? Is this worth going to prison?"

"Life is my prison," he said with a bitter smile. Then he jerked me to my bare feet. "Hold out your arms, Sharayah."

"No!" This was too familiar, as if the nightmare dream of Sharayah's was repeating itself, only by a different beach and with a different guy.

I screamed, but although my voice was strong, my arms weren't, and his fingers pressed fiercely, binding my wrists with tape. I struggled, overwhelmed with a sudden dizziness. I wondered if the tea I'd sipped had been drugged.

"Let me go!" I cried, fighting to stay clearheaded.

"It's your fault I have to get rough," he said, pushing me back against the seat. "I was going to make you fall in love with me first."

That confirmed it—he was insane.

"You can't just make someone love you," I argued.

"Oh, can't I?" He chuckled. "Saying things like 'you're different from other girls' is a good starter line. It's sad, really, how easy it is to manipulate naive girls. All it takes is some compliments, poetry and a romantic meeting. So I paid that kid a hundred bucks to attack you."

"That kid?" The room around me seemed to spin. "You mean ... Warren?"

"Right. It was all staged, of course, and he followed my script. I showed up just in time to rescue you, dazzle you with my heroics and look into your eyes in a way that left you longing for more. It was working, too. You wanted to see me again, didn't you?"

"No!" I lied, unwilling to give him that satisfaction. I'd been intrigued, grateful and eager to see Dyce again. But I'd also felt guilty, too, because how could I be attracted to Dyce when I had such a great thing started with Eli?

But now I find out his rescue was scripted! Unbelievable!

Warren's role in this was even more surprising. Why would a Dark Lifer care about money? Or could I have been wrong about Warren? The gloves may not have meant anything, simply been a bad fashion choice. Is that why my GEM told me he'd been returned to his "dwelling"?

"Don't deny it," Dyce was saying. "We both know you wanted me."

"I just want to get far away from you."

"That's not how you felt yesterday when I left you on the beach. You were so awed by my heroics you would have done anything I wanted." He said this in such an arrogant manner that if my hands weren't bound, I would have slapped the smile off his cocky-ass face.

Instead I spat at him.

"Damn you!" He jumped back, swearing and lifting his arm angrily.

I cringed, expecting his hand to smash down on me. But he used the back of his palm to wipe his cheek. "That was disgusting and crude. Why are you making everything so difficult? This would have gone so much smoother if you'd fallen in love with me like you did before."

"Before?" I gasped.

"I thought the wild girl behavior was fake and expected

213

that you'd be the same innocent soul that fell in love with Gabe. I brought you here planning to win your heart with gifts, poetry and romance. But you didn't even recognize my poetry. Then, instead of falling into my arms, you refused to even step on my boat." He scowled at me, as if it was my fault this kidnapping wasn't going well and I should apologize for ruining his plans.

Yeah, like that was going to happen. I scowled right back.

"I expected you to be grateful and malleable, not so defiant. Aren't you afraid of what I'm going to do?" he taunted. "I could take you far out to sea and dump you overboard. Then I would just leave you—like you did with Gabe."

I remained silent, too stubborn to give him the satisfaction of fear.

"No pleading or crying?" He studied me, his eyes under the brim of his hat slanted with curiosity. "Fine. I'm through here. This should hold you while I go up top."

In a swift movement, he ripped off a long strip of duct tape, splitting it with his teeth. He grabbed my legs with his other hand and forced tape around my ankles, so tightly I winced in pain. Then he peered down at me, as if waiting for me to plead with him to let me go. And I might have—except that something more startling caught my attention. I stared at Dyce's cheek and then his hand, a slow realization dawning.

His cheek where I'd spit had lightened in tone. When he'd rubbed the spot, his tan ... it must be tanning spray ... had worn off. Looking down, I saw that a bruise near his wrist was simply a patch of pale skin—and it was glowing an ominous gray.

Dyce was a Dark Lifer.

I swallowed my gasp, not wanting him to guess what I knew.

Still, I think he suspected something because he folded his arms across his chest and stared at me. I looked away, defiantly ignoring him although I watched from the corner of my eye. After a long, terrifying moment he shook his head, clearly puzzled but unable to figure me out. Then he turned abruptly and climbed up the stairs. When the trap door slammed shut, I sagged back on the bench.

I'd sent the DD Team after the wrong person.

Not Warren.

Dyce.

Small things suddenly made sense—like how I'd felt dizzy

whenever Dyce touched me. It wasn't lust, but a reaction to his dark energy. The tingly feeling had nothing to do with hormones or drugged tea; just being close to him made me weak, probably more than ordinary girls because I wasn't that different from him.

A temporary soul in someone else's body.

Did he know? How could he not know? When I met him, I must have been carrying the glowing energy Grammy told me about.

I thought about this but decided no, for whatever reason, he really didn't know. This wasn't about me being a Temp Lifer. Dyce's revenge was personal for Sharayah. He'd waited months to get her alone and vulnerable. He'd admitted to studying her interest in poetry, even her taste in food. But why was he so obsessed with her?

I thought about what I knew about Dark Lifers. They were non-living souls who'd gone on Temp Life missions—but instead of returning to the other side, they hid in unsuspecting bodies. They could borrow a body for a full moon's cycle unless an injury forced them out sooner. Then they had only minutes to find a new body or they'd glow like a neon sign flashing *Hey, DD Team! Come and get me!* Most Dark Lifers were newly deceased, inexperienced and hiding out because they were afraid. They usually made mistakes that led to their quick capture.

Seasoned Dark Lifers, though, had decades, even centuries of experience and continued to elude the DD Team. They were cunning and dangerous. Their forceful touch could drain victims of their energy and leave them empty.

Dyce was definitely not a newbie. I should have guessed

he wasn't a regular guy from his formal way of speaking and how he quoted famous dead people. For all I knew, he could be one of those famous dead people. His name probably wasn't even Dyce; that was just the body he currently inhabited. Did Dark Lifers use their own names or assume the role of their victims? Doing some quick math, I guessed that he would have been in three different bodies since Sharayah struggled with Gabe. He could have been posing as a college student, a professor or even one of the girls living in Sharayah's dorm. Ooh. Gross.

But kidnapping me was extreme to avenge a friend—unless Dyce was more than a friend to Gabe. And that's when I finally realized what was going on here.

Dyce wasn't just a friend of Gabe's.

Dyce *was* Gabe.

✳

The bad news: I was trapped with a Dark Lifer who thought I'd left him for dead and would most likely toss me into the ocean for shark food once we were far out at sea.

The good news: None.

I was doomed.

But despite having no ideas for escape, I had too much stubborn determination to give up. There had to be a way out of this.

So I racked my brain for every piece of information from every self-help book I'd ever read. The only thing I could come up with was from *Adversaries are Allies*. The advice was meant for business situations, like when your boss hates you. It was all about turning adversaries (people who hate you) into allies (loyal friends). One strategy involved creating two columns: one for your strengths and the other for your adversary's weakness. Then use your strengths to strike his weaknesses.

Hmmm, being tied up with duct tape didn't leave me with any strengths. But I was strong in knowledge, I realized. I knew he was a Dark Lifer, but he didn't know I was a Temp Lifer. He knew Sharayah had changed, but he had no idea how drastically. There had to be some advantage in knowing this... but what? And how could I do anything with my hands and legs taped together?

The GEM!

If I could just push it out of my pocket and open the pages, I could literally call for help. Grandma was only a page-turn away and she'd send in the DD Team. They'd kick Dyce-Gabe's arrogant ass out of his stolen body and back to the other side where he belonged.

Leaning back against the bench cushion, with my taped hands on my lap, I fumbled for the pocket in my skirt. When I felt the book beneath my taped wrists, I pushed it up. I leaned sideways to get the right angle, groaning as my legs, also taped together, twisted painfully. My hair flew in my face, swinging into my mouth. I spit it out, all the while working on the book. A corner of it poked out from the pocket. But to get it any farther out I'd have to be a contortionist, and I'd always hated exercise.

I'd just managed to twist almost completely upside down— my bound feet were wiggling above my head and my hands were a finger-touch away from the GEM—when the door to the cabin opened.

"Miss me?" Dyce called out cheerfully. "Hey, why are you upside down?"

I jerked upright, tossing my feet back to the ground and popping up in the seat like nothing unusual had happened.

"Trying to get circulation back into my feet," I said, breathing hard. "You wrapped them so tight."

"I'll unwrap them when we're on our way."

My pulse jumped. So we were going out to sea? *Doomed*, I thought again. I had to get out of here before we left the dock.

"Could you loosen my legs now?" I asked in a more cajoling tone. "It's not like there's anywhere I can run."

"True." He rubbed his chin thoughtfully. "But you're like a wire stretched tight, ready to snap. Are you up to something?"

"Nothing," I said, breathing fast.

He stepped closer, studying me suspiciously. "I don't believe you."

"What can I do with my hands and legs taped?"

"That's what I'm trying to figure out."

"Don't you ever believe anyone?"

"No. Why are you acting so nervous?"

"Um ... let me think. What do I have to be nervous about? Oh, yeah. I've just been kidnapped and have no idea what you plan to do to me." I listened for the tell tale sound of the boat's motor, but all was silent. At least we hadn't left the dock ... yet.

"You don't sound afraid. You sound like you're hiding something," he said, idly reaching up to adjust his cap as he studied me.

I really should have been terrified, but now that I was just a whisper away from using my GEM, I grew braver. "Sure, I have a semi-automatic weapon hidden in my hands."

He started for my hands, then realized I was mocking him and drew back with an expression I could only describe as embarrassment. "You're not in a position to make jokes."

"I'm not in a position to do much of anything."

"So why the sarcasm when you should be begging for mercy?" He pursed his lips tight. "Don't you realize what could happen to you?"

"Stuff happens. Like this book advised: *The rock that rolls with the flow reaches its goal quickly.* So why get all stressed out over something I have no control over?"

"That's very odd advice. What sort of book is that from?"

"*Bottom Feeders Rise to Stardom.*"

"That's an actual book?" He knelt down close to me. "Or are you joking again?"

"It's a book, but it's sort of dumb, more comedy than commonsense. I can't recite poetry like you, but I do know my self-help books."

"I thought you only read romance novels and poetry," he said in a puzzled tone.

"People change."

"But not this much. You look the same, but you move and talk like a different person."

"Like I care?" I snapped, hoping to irritate him so much he'd leave. "If you aren't going to let me go, get your ugly face out of here."

Instead of getting mad, he laughed. "So you think I'm ugly?"

"Hideous. I can't stand looking at you, so why don't you leave?"

He ignored my request, moving to check his reflection in a mirror mounted on a cabinet, turning his head right, then left, quizzically. "This is a pleasant face. Nice eyes, straight nose and good bone structure. I doubt other girls would complain."

"So kidnap another girl and let me go."

He laughed again. "Did you think Gabe was ugly, too?"

"Not at first, but lies and duct tape are real turn-offs."

Dyce turned from the table, studying me with a shiver-worthy intensity. "There's something unusual about you that I can't figure out. It's tempting to change my plans and keep you longer."

Keep me *alive* longer? Is that what he meant? I was all for staying alive, but running out of patience with this egotistical control freak and his obsessive talk about plans. What motivated him to hijack random bodies? Was he afraid of the unknown, a wacko psychopath, or did he just hate women? I was guessing number three because of his sick love-them-and-duct-tape-them routine.

"A penny for your thoughts, Sharayah," he said softly.

"You wouldn't like them."

"Still, I'd like to know."

"All I'm thinking is that I want to leave," I said wearily. Should I try to calmly reason with him or would tears be more likely to work?

"It will all be over soon," he added with a smile.

I did not like his smile. I did not like anything about him—especially the telltale glow shining from his hand. My gaze fixed on his hand as he reached up to push back a wet strand of hair, then followed it down to the table. Dyce idly drummed his fingers. The glowing seemed brighter now, a beacon drawing my gaze.

If only he would leave the room! I thought. Then I could send an SOS through the GEM. What had he meant when he said it would "be over soon"? If I didn't use the GEM immediately, I might never get a chance.

"I have to go pee," I announced, squirming for effect.

He scowled. "Can't it wait?"

"No."

"Nice try. You can manage on your own. The bathroom is right there." He pointed to a door which I'd assumed was a closet.

I shifted slowly, placing my bound feet on the ground, then standing up. I bunny-hopped a few feet, then wobbled.

"Don't fall—" Dyce jumped up to catch me.

"Nooooo!" I screamed as his Dark Lifer hands came toward me. "Stay away from me, Gabe!"

He stopped abruptly. "What did you call me?"

"Um … nothing." Steadying myself against the wall, I avoided his gaze. "I'll just hop over to the bathroom."

"Wait. Why did you call me Gabe?" He blocked my way.

"A slip of the tongue."

"It was more than that. What have you guessed, Sharayah?"

I faked confusion. "I don't know what you mean. We only met yesterday."

"You know better than that," he said softly.

"I only know that my arms and legs hurt, I want out of here, and I need to pee."

As I waited for him to answer, my gaze returned to the shiny patch on his hands. He caught my look, and glanced down and covered the shiny skin with his other hand.

"Who are you?" he demanded, sounding more confused than angry.

"That's a stupid question," I snapped. "You admitted to studying me for months, so you probably know me better than I do."

"I'm not so sure anymore."

He reached out toward my face with his arm—the one with the shiny patch—and I recoiled. "No! Don't touch me!"

"Why not?" he asked, moving closer.

"I-I just don't like being touched."

"Or could it be you don't like *my* touch?" he said, reaching out with both hands. "Tell me why."

His palms hovered so close that my pulse raced with fear.

"No!" I cringed, turning away.

"I'm going to place both of my hands on you and keep them there, pressing down harder and harder until you tell me the truth. Just like this—"

At the touch of his palms, I screamed, "Keep your Dark Lifer hands off me!"

My words seemed to steal the air from the room. Instantly Gabe pulled his hands back and went silent. Overwhelmed, I collapsed on the bench.

Gabe crossed to the table, sitting in a chair with his arms bent and his head resting against his hands. He sat like this for at least five minutes. The only sound was my quick breathing and an occasional drop of sea water slipping from his shirt to the floor. I wanted to kick myself, but of course I couldn't with my legs bound. I'd forgotten to act like Sharayah. Dumb, so dumb! I'd blundered big time. I'd thought that knowing his secret while he didn't know mine would give me power. But maybe I was looking at this the wrong way. Maybe the truth, as the saying goes, could literally set me free.

As long as I mixed in a good amount of lying.

"Okay, I admit it," I said. "I know what you are."

He arched one dark brow, his expression like stone. "What do you know about Dark Lifers?"

"They're renegade Temp Lifers but without energy from the other side, so their hands and fingernails are gray and glowing. I guessed that you sprayed on a tan to hide your glow."

"How does a mere girl know this?" he demanded.

"My grandmother told me."

"Your grandmother?" he repeated doubtfully. "I suppose you believe in the Big Bad Wolf and Humpty Dumpty, too."

I didn't appreciate his mocking tone. "FYI, my grandmother has an important job on the other side. And I know Dark Lifers are real because I've met one. He tried to hurt me, too, but I got rid of him."

"Oh?" Gabe looked doubtful. "And how did you do that?"

"I contacted the Dark Disposal Team."

His tanned face turned as pale as old bones. "You know about them?"

"Yes, and they'll be here soon." A method for telling a convincing lie that I'd learned from *Let's Fake a Deal*, a self-help book written by a top Hollywood agent, was to first convince yourself you were telling the truth. "The DDT will be here soon," I repeated.

As if my words had physically struck him, he stepped back from me. Then he shook his head. "I don't believe you."

"Then wait around to find out. But from what my grandmother tells me, you won't like what they do to Dark Lifers."

"Your grandmother is the overseer of the Temporary Lifer program?"

"Yeah, and even though she's dead she's very protective of me. She told me a secret way to let her know when I find a Dark Lifer. So you better scrap your plans for dumping me in the ocean and get out of here while you can."

"I've eluded capture for over a century and have no intention of returning now." He glared at me. "Do you have any idea what you've done?"

"I think so." I spoke calmly, but inside I quaked at the dark energy oozing from him. He'd been playing with me before—but now he was serious and angry.

"No, you don't. And you're wrong about my dumping you in the ocean. I would never hurt you. I'd planned to let you fall in love with me all over again, then explain to you how love is only a trap. Once you understood that love isn't real and learned to guard your heart, I would have let you go. I went through all of this to help you. I still care about you, Sharayah."

"Nothing says 'I love you' better than duct tape," I said with a sarcastic lift of my bound hands.

"I had to make sure you listened."

"You've confessed to sending me death threats and plotting revenge for what happened to Gabe...I mean, to you."

"Right," he admitted, his cap bobbing with his nod. "I'd never failed before that night, and at first I was angry. But that's only part of the reason I tracked you down. I had to finish what I started—to save you."

"Save me?" I almost choked. "From what?"

"From a life destroyed by false love. You fell in love with me too easily, quicker than most girls did. You were so eager for romance and so trusting that I knew someone would destroy you if I didn't teach you to be strong."

"By breaking my heart?" I asked incredulously.

"By showing you the true deception of love. That's all I wanted to do—convince you that true love doesn't exist."

"I don't believe that," I argued, thinking of Eli.

"You're still too trusting and naive. That's why I tried to prevent you from making the mistakes that I did."

"What mistakes?"

"When I was alive, I was betrothed to a sweet young lady. As was common with gentry in those days, I also had a mistress. I respected my betrothed but only had passion for my mistress. I would rather have lived in poverty than in wealth without her, so I planned to run away and marry her. Instead, she murdered my betrothed so that we wouldn't have to run. And since I still loved her and wanted to protect her, I confessed to her crime. She came to see me while I was in prison and laughed that I'd been a fool. She said that she had many men and only loved my family's money, never me. Everything that mattered died before I met the gallows. When I became a Dark Lifer, it wasn't out of fear—it was to save naive romantics from the destruction of love."

He seemed to be waiting, watching me for a reaction. But I wasn't sure what to say. His twisted logic chilled me, yet inspired some sympathy, too. I mean, going to the gallows for someone you loved was tragic.

"I'm sorry that you died and everything," I said after what seemed like a long stretch of silence. "The DDT will be here any minute."

"You shouldn't have contacted them."

"You shouldn't have taped me up."

"I did it for your own good. In one hundred and twenty years, you are my only failure. I regret not helping you, Sharayah," he said sadly.

Then a shift took place in his expression, as if he was realizing something he'd forgotten until now. "But you aren't Sharayah. Are you?"

I hesitated, then shook my head.

"Who are you?"

Lying seemed a waste of time, so I went with the truth. "Amber."

"A Temp Lifer?" he guessed.

"Yes. Sent to repair the damage you did to Sharayah by letting her think she'd killed you. What really happened that night?"

"I was getting ready to give my speech about deceitful love. After that I always walked away, knowing they'd be wiser now. Only Sharayah ruined it and I fell. I missed the rocks but suffered bad cuts. Do you know what happens to Dark Lifers if they bleed?"

"They can't stay in the body very long."

"Right, and have to immediately find a new one," he explained. "I hitched a ride and switched with the guy who picked me up. Unfortunately, the car was a hot one and I got arrested. I spent three stinking, disgusting, humiliating weeks in jail."

"Am I supposed to feel sorry for you?"

"Not sympathy, but respect for my attempts to reach you. I never gave up trying to find you, even though it took weeks. Finally I found you in San Jose and slipped into the body of a young man residing in a nearby dorm."

Something clicked. "Was his name Caleb, and did he go out with a girl named Katelyn?"

"Very good," he said, impressed.

"What about the real Gabe?" I asked. "Is he really paralyzed?"

"I'm the only real Gabe—my name is Gabriel Deverau—but I suppose you mean the body I used when I dated Sharayah. What was his real name?" He touched his chin thoughtfully. "Well, no matter. He only has a few memories of my time in his body. Aside from some cuts and confusion, he walked away to resume his safe, boring life. And now I must resume my lives, too."

I cringed at his use of "lives" plural. He was a menace and would keep breaking hearts unless he was stopped. Still, I was relieved that he didn't have any plans to drown me.

"The DD Team will never catch me," he said as he started up the stairs.

"You're just leaving?" I cried, thrashing my bound hands and legs. "What about me?"

"The DD Team can set you free."

Then he was gone.

Oh, great.

I'd lied to Gabe so convincingly that he'd left without untaping me.

Still, I could turn my "lie" into the truth easily enough.

Bending sideways, I reached for my GEM again.

It took awhile to push it out of my pocket with just my fingertips, but after a lot of groaning and twisting, I was rewarded with a thump on the floor. The GEM flipped over twice, then fell open to a beautiful blank page.

Before I'd finished asking for the DD Team and explaining where I was, there was a startling flash and four members of the DD Team, wearing business suits, squished into the tiny cabin. Gabe must be high on their *Wanted, Dead and Alive* list for them to send in four team members.

They didn't waste any time, either, uncoiling their silver ropes as they surrounded me. Their rapid-fire questions made me dizzy: What did the Dark Lifer look like? Did he give a name? Where did he go? I did my best to answer but I couldn't tell them much. And I grew increasingly uncomfortable, squished like a badly wrapped gift against the bench cushions.

Finally I couldn't take it anymore.

"Enough questions!" I interrupted. "Would someone please untape me?"

✱

A short time later, wearing only one shoe and the clothes from Gabe, I hobbled back to Club Revolution.

About a mile away, I felt the vibrations in the air and the ground and saw the beautiful sight of bright lights blazing against the backdrop of the dark, misty night.

Then I turned a corner and saw the most wonderful sight in the entire world.

Eli—running toward me.

I ran, too, so full of emotion that I didn't even think about what I looked like or who I was when I threw my arms around him.

"I'm so glad to see you!" I cried, burying my face in his jacket.

"Amber! I've been searching everywhere and was ready to call the police. Where have you been?"

I shook my head, too tired and cold to think about anything except how good it felt to be in his arms.

"You're freezing. Here, take my coat," he offered.

But I shook my head, remembering Gabe/Dyce giving me his jacket. "Just hold me," I whispered. "Oh, Eli! I'm so glad to be back with you."

"What happened?"

"It was Dyce...I mean Gabe. He-he lied and then tried to kidnap me." I held out my hands, which were raw and red under the shining street lights.

"Bastard! Where is he? I'll go there and—"

"And what?" I almost laughed at his ferocious tone; it was like he was a Chihuahua ready to take on a wolf, which was so sweet that I almost cried. "It's okay now. He's gone for good."

"Are you all right? Should we call the police?"

"Already taken care of," I said, not having the energy to go into all the details.

"But what happened? I don't understand any of this."

"I'll explain later," I promised. "Now I just want to be held."

And kissed, I thought.

He must have been thinking the same thing, because he pulled me closer and tipped my chin, his touch so gentle, making me feel safe and warm. Not the tingling thrill of Gabe's touch, but so much more real and honest. I could trust Eli with my life and my heart. You're wrong about love, Gabe, I thought.

Smiling for the first time in hours, I looked into Eli's eyes and lifted my lips toward his—until we heard a gasp and jumped apart.

Turning around, I saw Sadie staring at us with the most disgusted look I'd ever seen on her face.

"Ohmygod, Rayah!" she exclaimed. "Kissing your own brother! That's just sick!"

∗

It took some fast talking, but Sadie eventually believed that we weren't kissing (which was true, since she'd so rudely interrupted) and that Eli was just comforting me because I'd been kidnapped. Showing Sadie my bruised wrists and ankles added proof.

After that, things were kind of a blur. Sadie talked a lot, relieved I wasn't going to call the police, then told me she'd run into Warren but he'd blown her off. She'd called him some appropriate names and told him where he could go. Then she met a new guy who was way better than Warren, anyway.

When I asked about Mauve, Sadie shrugged and said she was back with Alonzo. Apparently, for the first time in Mauve's history, she was trying monogamy. I had my doubts but hoped it worked for her.

Eli wanted me to stay with him at his friends' house but I didn't want to have to make small talk with strangers. He promised to pick me up early (in about six hours) for the *Voice Choice* audition, then he dropped me off at the crappo condo.

My bed and Kitty Calico were waiting for me.

When I awoke, I was surprised to see Mauve sleeping on the fold-out bed and the cat now cuddled up to her (traitor!). I shut off the alarm, so groggy I was tempted to forget about the audition and sleep all day. But I couldn't let Sharayah down. In less than twelve hours I'd return to my own body, and she'd have to survive on her own—which would be much easier if she made the *Voice Choice* finals.

After a quick shower, I sorted through Sharayah's clothes to find something that would attract attention and wow the judges. I found a bright red stretchy top and matched it with a cropped, bead-trimmed denim jacket, black jeans and black half-boots. My hair was a mess, so I twisted it into a messy bun that gave me kind of a rebel-rocker look. Keeping with this theme, I applied heavy amounts of kohl eye makeup, autumn-brown eye shadow and ruby-death-ray lipstick.

I thought leaving at six would be early enough, but by the time Eli got off the congested freeways and found a parking space, the line-up for the competition was like a mile long. No exaggeration!

"What do they think this is?" I complained to Eli as I took my sorry position at the end of the line. "American Idol?"

"Looks like it," he agreed. "But we've made it this far. We can wait."

I gave him a surprised look. "You don't have to stay with me. It could be hours."

"I don't mind." He grinned and slipped his arm casually around my shoulders. "I'm just being a supportive brother."

"Oh, brother," I sighed, but I was grinning, too.

I'd always enjoyed people-watching, and waiting in that line gave me plenty to watch. Most auditioners had come prepared with chairs, blankets, pillows and coolers. One girl was actually sleeping on a folding cot, her friends shifting it a few inches whenever the line moved—which wasn't often.

One hour, then two, then three went by before I was close enough to see the front of the line. But it was still about a block—and a few hundred people—away. By hour four, though, I was feeling better because Eli had gone out for hamburgers, drinks and fries, returning with a blanket, too.

As we were finishing our food, a guy in a black cap (that had a microphone logo and *VC* on the front) came by with legal forms to complete. He started to hand one to Eli, but "my brother" shook his head and gestured to me. Since I didn't know Sharayah's address or other personal details, I handed the form and pen to Eli. The line started to move again, so he hastily filled out the form, then handed it to the *VC* official a few minutes later.

Then we stood for another hour with no line movement at all. It was so frustrating, being this close yet still not inside. Eli and I passed the time by planning what song I would sing. I wanted to go with something bluesy to show off Sharayah's vocal range, but Eli thought I should do something off the latest Top Ten. We argued for about three feet's worth of line movement before settling on something that was bluesy but also popular.

As we waited, doubts began to strike me. All around, singing hopefuls belted out their songs, some dancing, too. But what had I done to prepare? Nothing. I still wasn't sure about my song choice, which was the most important thing. How could I possibly have any chance at winning?

As I was thinking I should just give up now and leave, the line started moving again. Much faster. For the first time since arriving I could actually see the entry door. Double doors, actually, with official security guards grilling each person before allowing them to go inside. Someone in a bear outfit had just stepped in, followed by triplet guys all dressed in black and then a girl who could double for Britney Spears. When I counted the people in front of me, there were only twenty-five.

"Excuse me," someone said behind me.

I turned and saw a gray-haired woman, her face wrinkled and her frail body stooped over. She wore a pleated navy-blue skirt, a long-sleeved blue blouse and a yellow scarf. I'd never seen her before, so wondered why she'd come over to me.

"Yes?" I asked curiously, since there was an age restriction in the contest rules disqualifying anyone over thirty, and this withered old woman had to be at least thirty times three.

"I wondered if you could spare some water," she asked weakly, pointing to the water bottles Eli had bought earlier. "So many hours waiting...and I'm feeling dizzy. I can pay you."

Eli reached out and handed her a bottle. "You can have it, no charge," he said.

"Thank you so much. I knew just by looking at you two youngsters that you were kind."

"Are you here for the competition?" I asked.

"Only to support my talented grandson. But after a visit to the ladies room, I've lost him. He must have gone inside but the guards won't let me in."

"They won't?" Eli said with a fierce frown. "Well, I'll see about that. Come with me and I'll talk to them for you."

"That's sweet of you, but I don't mind waiting." She waved her hand a bit helplessly. "Although it's getting so warm and I'm—" Her voice broke off and her feet buckled.

We both moved to help but Eli reached her first, cradling her in his arms so she didn't fall. He grabbed a water bottle, twisted it open and held it up to her mouth. "Take a sip," he encouraged gently.

"That's better…but, ooh…everything is spinning." She stood up and took a step forward then swayed.

"You need medical attention," Eli said firmly. "I'll talk to the guards and see if there's a medic nearby."

"Gracious, no. I don't want anyone fussing over me. I'll be fine if I just take a moment in the ladies' room."

"I'll take you there," Eli offered.

She shooed him away. "Young men have no place going near a ladies' room. I'll be fine."

But it was obvious by the way she wobbled that she couldn't make it two feet on her own.

"I'll take you," I offered.

"You can't leave now," Eli protested.

"This won't take long, and you can hold my place for me. The restroom isn't far and I can get back before the line moves." Not giving Eli a chance to argue, I stood and took the frail woman by the arm.

She moved surprisingly quickly once we neared the restroom. When I reached for the door, I frowned at an *out of service* sign hanging on the knob. "Oh, no. We'll have to find another place."

"Don't mind that," she said, pushing the door open. "I was here earlier and it works just fine." Then she wobbled, and I lunged forward to keep her from falling.

The bathroom seemed to be in working order: no leaking faucets or overflowing toilets. I led the woman to a stall. She leaned against the door and reached into her shoulder bag.

"I'm going to go now," I said as I turned around.

"No, you aren't. You're staying here with me." She whipped something gray out of her bag and aimed it at me.

A stun gun.

As I stared in astonishment, she reached up and yanked off her gray wig. Shining red curls tumbled down over her not-so-old shoulders.

Too shocked to think, I said the first thing that popped into my head. "What is it with you and bathrooms?"

"It was the only place to get you alone."

"I can't believe you followed me over four hundred miles! Are you obsessed or something? What's this all about?" I was trying to stall her while I gauged the distance between the door and her gun hand, considering my chances for rushing her. I was taller than she was by at least six inches, but she was wider and probably stronger. I could run faster... but not faster than her trigger finger.

"No sudden moves." She kept the gun aimed at me. "I don't want to use this, but I will if you don't do exactly what I say."

I nodded, fear creeping up my spine. "What do you want?"

"My best friend back the way she used to be," she said with a weary sigh. "Sharayah, this is an intervention."

23

"I've missed you so much, Shari," the redhead continued, so miserably that even though she held the stun gun, I felt a little sorry for her.

Best friend? I remembered Eli telling me how Sharayah dumped all her friends, even her closest friend since childhood.

"Hannah?" I guessed.

"I followed you hundreds of miles and borrowed my mother's Taser just to get you alone." She wiped tears from her eyes with her free hand. "I even went to this funky Taser party with my mom to learn how to use this. I'm not kidding around, Shari, I will stun you if that's what it takes to keep you here."

"But I have to get back to the audition. I was almost to

the front of the line and there isn't much time left before—" I hesitated, realizing this wasn't the time or place to explain about Temp Lifers. "Anyway, this competition is really important."

"Other things are more important ... like our friendship."

"Hannah, I know you're a wonderful friend, but I really need to go back to Eli. Can't we just meet after the competition?"

"To hell with the goddamned competition!" Then she blushed, as if ashamed by her outburst. "See how crazy you make me? I almost never swear because of how we think it's so demeaning. Remember when we found that Shakespearean-insult website and went around saying stuff like 'thou crusty beef-witted canker blossom' and 'thou poisonous fly-bitten fustilarian'? We mocked other kids who only repeated the same boring swear words. But you've changed ... I can't believe what I've been hearing about you."

That's for sure, I thought ruefully. I nodded to show her I was ashamed, then subtly took a step closer to the door.

"Stop!" she ordered, with a steady aim of the gun. "I'm way serious about this intervention."

"I have to g—"

"Don't interrupt! I've gone through hell because of you, and the least you can do is give me fifteen freaking minutes of your time. I don't want to hear any more arguments. Be quiet and listen until we're done ... or else." She pushed the gun closer to me.

I lifted my hands in surrender. "I'll stay," I promised.

She exhaled so deeply that the faux wrinkles on her face relaxed. Now that I could see her close up, I was embarrassed that I'd been fooled by the grandma act. Her reddish-brown lashes curled over large chocolate eyes that were glistening with emotion. But her full lips were pressed together with determination as she kept a steady grip on the gun.

"You have to do what I say." She reached behind her for a cheerful blue beach bag and pulled out a small blanket. She tossed it on the floor and told me to spread it out, then sit down.

Impressed with how far she'd gone to help a friend—and not wanting to give her any reason to try out that Taser—I obediently sat down. Hannah's granny skirt flared out on the blanket as she sat down across from me, keeping her gun hand lifted while she grabbed the straps of her bag and swung it between us.

"This is how this works." She spoke with determination. "You sit still and look at what I have to show you. No interruptions."

"But what about Eli? He'll worry when I don't come back."

"I'll take care of him." She withdrew a phone from her bag, then flipped it open with her pink-frosted thumbnail. It was a smooth move, actually, since her other hand continued to hold the gun. I couldn't help but be impressed with her multitasking skills.

Except I was more anxious about what she was going to do. I watched uneasily while she punched a button and lifted the phone to her ear.

"Hey, Eli," she said in a casual tone. "Yeah, it's Hannah...I know, it is a surprise...actually, that's why I'm calling." The gun wiggled as she laughed. "She's here with me, it's a coincidence but we just ran into other...Calm down, she's fine, but she's having severe stage fright so I'm giving her a pep talk. She says for you to go ahead and she'll join you soon." Abruptly, Hannah hung up.

"All done," she told me, smiling. I noticed that as she put her phone away, she hit the *off* button.

"So now what?" I asked warily.

"The intervention begins." She used the butt end of the gun to gesture to her beach bag. "We'll start with our sixth-grade science trip."

✳

When she started pulling out scrapbooks and photo albums, I began to think Hannah's bag was a bottomless pit. She had each of her many books organized with labels for the year and for the events. The blue album showed Hannah and Sharayah, age eleven, grinning as they paddled canoes and trudged on hikes at science camp. It was cute how they both wore pigtails and similar clothes, and even their poses were alike as they goofed for the camera.

Seeing them together made me think of Alyce and miss her more than ever. We'd never shared science camp (well, I'd gone, but even in elementary school Alyce shunned social events), but we did camp out once in a house that was rumored to be haunted. We hadn't met any ghosts but we scared each other by telling stories all night.

Album by album, I went back down Sharayah's memory lane. Sharayah and Hannah had been so close that I began to understand Hannah's motivation in bringing me here. And her resourcefulness was amazing. I mean, the "closed" sign on the bathroom was brilliant. No one would come in to disturb us.

Including Eli.

My mind wandered while she pointed to a picture of a golden, long-haired puppy that Sharayah had given her as a birthday gift when she turned sixteen. But each minute we reminisced diminished my hopes of winning the *Voice Choice* competition. I was running out of time—in more ways than one. The clock on my body switch was ticking, too. I wasn't wearing a watch so I didn't know the exact time, but I'd glanced at Eli's watch before I left him and it was almost three.

The body switch could happen soon.

Grammy had said that once it started, there was no stopping the process.

"Hannah, I've seen enough photos," I said as I closed a book from third grade. "I appreciate all you've done, and it's worked. This was exactly what I needed to get my head together. You're a great friend."

"That's not what you said when you moved out of our dorm. You cut me off like I was a stranger," she said with a sniff. "That was just cruel."

"I'm really sorry. But I wasn't myself—it was like I was possessed by a demon," I added for dramatic effect. Sharayah probably wasn't the dramatic type, but it always worked for me. "I was horrible, and you're the best friend in the universe not to give up on me. I can never thank you enough."

"Do you mean it?"

"Absolutely. I want to be friends again."

"Oh, Shari, that's what I was hoping you'd say." Her whole demeanor changed and she lowered her hand—but still held on to the gun. "I was sure all I needed to do was get you to listen to me and remember the good times."

"You were right," I assured. "Your intervention was a success. Since we're done here, I really need to get back to the contest."

"Why?" She wrinkled her brow.

"To show the judges what an amazing voice I have. Don't you want me to be a singing star?"

"You're joking, right?"

"Um ... no."

"Come off it, Shari. You're the most private person I know. You've never sung in public! You're always teasing Eli about his secret passion for karaoke. And you never, ever brag about having a good voice."

"So singing isn't my dream?" I asked.

"Duh. You can't stand pop tarts like Britney. You want to be a doctor." She frowned at me. "Maybe you really have been taken over by a demon. But I won't give up on you. I still have three photo albums and the scrapbook for the secret club we made when we were in third grade."

She eyed me suspiciously and lifted the Taser.

Then, with steely determination, she picked up yet another photo album.

While she turned pages and reminded me of a trip to Lake Tahoe and a wild ride on a snowmobile, my hands started to itch. The itch heated up into a strange warmth that spread through my arms. I glanced down and had to swallow a gasp when I saw my fingers glowing. And the rest of me felt weird, too. My thoughts swam in a fog and I felt numb all over, as if I was disconnecting from my body.

Sharayah's body.

What time was it? I tried to ask Hannah, panicked when

I couldn't hear my voice. Sounds echoed all around me, as if I were being swept along a dark tunnel.

It was happening, I realized. What I'd wished for desperately, yet dreaded, too. I was leaving Sharayah and returning home. Only I wasn't ready yet. I sent my thoughts out to Grammy, begging for more time because I hadn't made Sharayah a star. I hadn't said good-bye to Eli, either. It was all happening too fast, out of control, swirling dark colors mingling with a sense of rushing movement.

Then I felt myself stop.

A jolt as if I'd crashed into a wall.

And when I opened my eyes and looked around, I realized the "wall" wasn't made of brick or concrete—it was made of flesh, blood, and curly brown hair.

I was Amber again.

24

"**A**mber! You're awake!"

I glanced around, aware of so many things at once: the hospital bed I was in, the tube running from my arm to an IV pole, the half-open curtain letting in dim light from a cloudy day, and the crying woman staring down at me. After being in two different bodies within the past week, facing Dark Lifers and almost becoming the next *Voice Choice* star, I was me again. Average-looking, savvy, future entertainment agent Amber Borden.

"Mom?" I whispered, almost afraid to believe this was really happening.

My mother sobbed and rushed for the bed. Crying my name over and over (which was very cool to hear again!), she wrapped her arms gently around me, tears streaming down her cheeks and falling on my arm—an arm with faint scars from falling in nettles. Memories rushed back at me but this time they were my own: the screech of tires of a runaway mail truck, meeting Grammy Greta on the other side, waking up in the hospital in the wrong body.

But now, for the first time in weeks, I was in the right body.

And my mommy was hugging me.

Soon we were both crying.

It was like someone shook up a bottle of craziness, then popped open the cork. Everything blurred in a rush of joy and tears. Dad showed up, then nurses and doctors. Mom was like a bull charging up to the doctors, insisting that I was awake, healthy and ready to go home. While Mom battled about protocol and hospital rules, Dad bent down and hugged me so hard that a nearby machine started beeping. And throughout this, I kept studying my body, marveling at my freckles, small breasts, and chubby thighs.

I loved being me.

At some point during the insanity, a phone rang and my father handed it to me.

"Dustin!" I exclaimed.

"Amber?" he asked cautiously. "Is it really you?"

"Yes! But how did you find out already?"

"I have my sources," he said in his typical know-it-all tone. "Wow! You sound like the real you again."

"Great, huh?" I heard myself and smiled.

"Supreme greatness. So when can I see you?"

"Soon, I hope." I glanced over at my mother, who was

glaring furiously and arguing with a doctor. "My parents are working on getting me released ASAP."

"So you'll come home tomorrow?"

"I think so. Home—what a beautiful word."

"I'll bet it is. So chill and enjoy being back, but then I want to know everything. Like, how did the audition go?"

"Don't ask." My smile faded.

"You bombed?"

"Worse. I never made it. But I can't talk about that here," I added in a whisper. "I'll explain later."

"Call me when you're home."

"I will," I promised.

"And Amber, just so you know . . . " he paused, suddenly awkward.

"Yes?"

"It's great to have you—the real you—back."

I looked around at my parents and swelled with emotion. "I know."

✴

After a long night of tests and examinations, I was released the next morning. My little sisters tackled me when I walked through the front door, a tiny team of triplet football players wearing protective plastic trainer pants.

"Sissy, Sissy, Sissy!" Melonee, Olive, and Cherry screamed as they grabbed my legs and hugged.

I winced at the pain from my bruises (I had been hit by a truck, after all), but hugged them back. I couldn't get over how they'd grown. I was like Rip Van Winkle returning home after a hundred years, although it had been less than two weeks. But a few weeks for little kids is like a century. My sisters had learned new words and could string some together in short sentences. They each had new talents to show me. Olive could do a backward somersault (obviously not taking after her gym-resistant big sister), Melonee could count to eleven, and Cherry kept saying "Knock, knock," then giggling whenever I said, "Who's there?"

I was thrilled to see my cat Snowy, but she wasn't as friendly as Kitty Calico and gave me attitude (until dinner, when I snuck food to her under the table). Mom made a welcome-home, triple-layer caramel cream cake for me, and I showed my gratitude by taking two slices. Afterward, feeling sleepy and full, I went to my room—where I finally found some alone-time to make an important phone call.

Eli, Eli! Answer!

But he didn't.

The stupid phone rang and rang until the voicemail picked up. Where was Eli? I agonized. Why hadn't he answered? By now he must have realized I'd switched back to myself, so he should have tried to call me. Yet he hadn't.

Discouraged, I left a short "Call me ASAP!" message.

Then I tried Alyce's number.

I was still reeling with regret over not being there when she needed me. But now I was home and I would help her through her crisis—no matter what it was. It wouldn't be guy troubles, since she was too picky to go out with anyone. So that left either school/homework issues, complications with graveyard photographing, or something to do with her mother.

Usually her problems were mother-related.

So when her mother answered my call, I got a sick feeling in my gut.

"Hello…Is Alyce there?" I asked nervously. "This is Amber."

"I know who you are," she said coolly. What did she have against me, anyway? I'd always been extremely nice and polite to her.

"Can I talk to Alyce?" I asked.

"Why would you want to do that?" Her hostility was sharp enough to draw blood.

"Because I'm her best friend."

"My daughter has no friends."

"That's not true!" I argued. "Please tell her I want to talk to her."

"Unfortunately, she doesn't want to talk to you."

Click. Dead phone.

Oh, great, I thought grimly. That went well … *not*.

I stared at the phone in my hand, blaming myself for handling that all wrong. But what else could I have said? Did Alyce really hate me or was her mother lying? I thought back to our last conversation, how insistent Alyce was that I come home right away, then her anger when I'd refused. She'd needed me and I'd let her down.

Was our friendship really over?

Reaching across the bed, I scooped up my cat before she could protest and hugged her to my chest, a tear trickling down my cheek and landing on her silvery fur. If only I could read Alyce's mind to know what was wrong. She wouldn't talk to me, so how could I help her? I didn't dare go to her house now. Not when Attila the Horrible Mom might answer the door and slam it right in my face. But I could try at school. Alyce and I shared classes, so she couldn't ignore me forever. Somehow I'd fix everything and we'd be BFFs again.

The phone rang, and I grabbed it.

"Alyce?" I cried, hopefully.

"Sorry to disappoint you," came an amused male voice.

"Oh, Eli! I'm the opposite of disappointed," I assured him, sitting up and further disturbing Snowy, who hissed at me and indignantly scampered over to the edge of the bed. "I've been worried about you ... and Sharayah."

"Don't worry about me," he said. "And Sharayah seemed okay when she called a few hours ago. She's with Hannah."

"She is?" I relaxed against my pillow. "That's a relief. I worried about what happened after I left, but Sharayah will be fine with Hannah. I think Hannah is great—despite the stun gun."

"Stun gun?"

"A Taser. I'll tell you everything when I see you. Are you back home?"

"Not yet."

"Well, hurry! It'll be so cool to be with you and be myself. We can ... " I hesitated. "Well, finish what we started without breaking any moral or legal laws."

"I'd like that—but it could take awhile. There's something you should know about the *Voice Choice* competition."

"Oh ... that." I frowned. "Sorry I bailed on you but I couldn't help it. Hannah forced me into an intervention."

"What?"

"You know, an intervention. It's usually for someone on

drugs, or alcoholics, but Hannah did it to remind me—I mean, Sharayah—of their friendship. She had all these albums and—"

"That's really interesting," he interrupted. "But something major has happened that you need to know about."

"What?" I gripped the phone, imagining illness, car accidents and Dark Lifers.

"Relax, it's nothing bad. It's ridiculous, really," he said with an odd laugh. "I mean, I never expected anything like this to happen. I only stayed in line because I thought you were coming back. When I handed in the form, which I'd filled out fast and sloppy, they saw the name Rockingham and kept calling me 'Rocky.' Before I could explain, these official dudes led me to a stage, handed me a mike, and told me to start singing."

"Oh, poor Eli! How embarrassing!"

"It was at first, but all my goofing off with karaoke kicked in and I had fun."

"You're just being nice so I won't feel guilty for leaving you in such an awful situation. I'm so sorry I ever made you take me to that contest."

"Don't be sorry. I'm not, and neither were the judges." He chuckled. "I made it to the finals."

25

It was strange and wonderful to fall asleep in my own bed
and my real body that night. Although it was hard to
sleep with my mind spinning so fast, going over everything
that had happened. Some of it was good—like being with
my family and seeing my own face in a mirror. There was
also Eli's accidental success. Who knew he had a fabulous
voice? I was happy for him, but disappointed for myself
because he had to stay in L.A. for a week.

But it was Sharayah I couldn't forget. I was worried that
my mission to help her was incomplete. I'd been wrong about
her dreams and almost set her up for a competition she would
have hated. And I didn't restore her self-esteem or mend her
broken heart. There hadn't been enough time to even leave her

a letter of encouragement. The only thing I'd left behind was my GEM. What would she think when she found it? Would she remember anything that had happened the last few days? If she did, how would she handle knowing that Gabe was a Dark Lifer?

Not well, I suspected, which made me feel even worse. I had to be the worst Temp Lifer in history. If Sharayah did gain self-esteem and return to being a loving sister, loyal friend and top student, the credit would go to Hannah. Not me.

Sharayah was lucky to have a best friend who stuck by her no matter what and never gave up on their friendship. That's the kind of friendship I used to have with Alyce. But by not being there when Alyce needed me, I'd let her down.

Would she ever forgive me?

Tossing in my bed, I finally drifted off to sleep.

But somewhere in the middle of dreaming, I found myself surrounded by light and moving as if on an invisible escalator. I was rising up, up ... until I was stepping into a surreal world where a path of silvery clouds led me to Grandma Greta.

Cola was there, too, sitting on what seemed to be a comfortable leather couch, his Duty Director lit up like holiday lights. He barked and rushed over, tail wagging. I hugged him, enjoying the tickles of his doggy tongue on my face. Then I looked up at Grammy, tensing because I was afraid of what she'd say about my first (and last) Temp Lifer mission.

So I said it for her.

"I know, I know ... I blew it. I'm so sorry I let you down, Grammy."

"You haven't let anyone down," she told me. "You fulfilled your duties splendidly."

"But I didn't improve Sharayah's life."

"The Nine Divine Rules clearly state that a Temp Lifer is to live their Host Soul's life—not change it. You performed well. I'm very proud of you."

"Proud?" I rubbed my head, wondering if maybe this was a dream after all and not an actual experience. I'd been so sure I'd messed up. How could Grammy think I'd done a good job?

"Amber, you should be proud of yourself, too," she said as she opened her arms and pulled me against her warm, solid body. "You worked hard to follow the rules. Even though you bent them a little, it was all done for the right reasons."

"But I tried so hard to get Sharayah to the singing competition and failed. Then I found out she didn't want to be a star, she wants to work in a hospital and cure cancer. So I did absolutely nothing to make her dreams come true."

"Sharayah has many talents and plenty of time to fulfill her own dreams. You gave her the rest she needed, so that now she has the strength to make the right choices. It's her brother who has secret dreams of singing stardom." Grammy touched my hair softly. "And that's only one of many dreams you'll share with him."

There were subtle hints in her words that thrilled me. But asking about Eli's future felt like cheating, given that I hoped to be part of it. So I asked if Sharayah was going to be okay.

"Better than okay." Grammy led me over to the couch. We sat down and Cola curled up beside us. "She's ready to tackle her life again now."

"Will she remember everything that happened?"

"She'll remember what's important."

"Does that include Gabe?"

"She knows he's alive and that she shouldn't feel guilty." Grammy smiled at me. "You were wonderful, honey. Not many first-time Temp Lifers could handle a Dark Lifer."

"But I was wrong about Warren."

"You weren't that wrong—he had come in contact with a Dark Lifer. And thanks to you, we gained more information about Gabriel Deverau. He's the DD Team's most wanted Dark Lifer. You were very brave to stand up to him."

"I didn't feel brave. I felt scared." And strangely attracted, I thought guiltily.

"Don't worry—he will be caught. So next time you go on a mission, you won't have to worry about running into him."

"Next time? Not me." I shook my head adamantly. "I'm looking forward to finishing school, planning college and hanging out with my family and friends. Now that I sort of have a boyfriend, I may even go to prom. There are so many things I can't wait to do. I'm glad you think I did a good job, but I need to live my own life now. Besides, having me hospitalized has been really hard on my family. No more comas or strangers sleeping in my body."

"I understand," she said, with a sigh that seemed to form in a cloudy puff and linger in the air for a moment before vanishing. "It's just that I thought you'd want to help your friend."

"What friend?" I asked cautiously.

"Alyce."

"No way!" I felt my eyes would pop out, I was so shocked.

Then my grandmother began to explain that Alyce was in crisis mode and needed a time-out from life. Grammy wouldn't reveal what the problem was due to confidentiality rules, but she hinted that it was traumatic and a Temp Lifer would be assigned right away.

"Too bad you're not interested," she said with a shrug. "I'll find someone else to take the job."

"But you can't just put a stranger inside Alyce," I argued. "She's my best friend. I know her better than anyone."

She arched a brow. "You already told me you weren't interested, and I respect that. I wouldn't expect you to leave your body again … although I could make this exchange without interfering with your life. No coma or hospital."

"You could do that?"

"I can do many things," she said mysteriously. "And when you returned to your body, your friendship with Alyce would be better, too."

"Alyce will be okay?"

"With your help," Grammy said.

"She's my very best friend in the world. I'd do anything to help her."

"Are you accepting this mission?"

"Can you promise me that my body won't be stuck in a hospital again and that I won't miss any more school?"

"It's a promise. While you're absent from your body, I'll arrange a temporary occupant."

"Occupant!" Horrified, I stared at her. "But I don't want a Temp Lifer in my body! That's just too creepy."

"Not a Temp Lifer. It'll be someone you can trust and who loves you more than is humanly possible."

"Who?" I asked warily.

Grammy pointed to herself. "Me."

I slipped from my cloudy conversation with Grammy into a calm, floating sensation so peaceful that all my fears faded away. Grammy said the change would be immediate, so I imagined my soul like a flame of energy, shooting from the other side down to the quiet street where Alyce and her mother lived in a brown, L-shaped corner house.

This switch wouldn't be a shock like it was with Leah Montgomery, or confusing like it was with Sharayah. This time I knew exactly who I would be, and except for Alyce's recent issues, we shared all our secrets. Sometimes I felt that we were so close we were like twins, although we looked completely different. I was freckled with curly brown hair, and Alyce had exotic long black hair and golden-brown skin. I knew all her favorite things, her school schedule, her teachers, her friends and enemies. Once I found out what her problem was, I'd solve it and our friendship would be better than ever. It would be strange to see myself with Grammy's soul living my life, but cool, too.

Being Alyce for a few days would be the easiest Temp Lifer assignment ever.

So I sailed free and gave myself whole-heartedly into my mission.

I imagined her bedroom at the back of their house, where an oak tree brushed up against the window, creaking eerily in strong winds and offering climbing branches for when Alyce needed to sneak out at night, or for when I wanted to visit without her mother knowing. I could almost feel the force of movement as dreams and reality blended and I neared my destination.

Then everything slowed. I had a sense of weight, as if I were a heavy stone and falling, falling until a jolt rocked me and I felt substance again. There was a gradual awareness of arms, hands, legs and Alyce's silky black hair. I was lying on my back on silky fabric with my arms pressed against my sides.

I willed my eyes open ... then realized they were open. Only I was encased in total darkness.

I knew Alyce's house almost as well as I knew my own, and realized with growing alarm that while I seemed to be in Alyce's body, I was not in her bedroom. The air was stuffy, with an overwhelming fragrance of woodsy pines and flowers. Not the natural outdoors, either, but artificial, like the spray from an aerosol can.

And when I moved my borrowed arms and legs, I banged into a hard solid surface. Lifting my head, I bumped it against a low ceiling. No, not a ceiling, I realized, as I ran Alyce's fingers over a smooth, rounded surface. I was trapped somewhere dark and confining.

As my eyes started to adjust, I noticed tiny pricks of light at the edges around me. A growing horror was building inside me and I shivered. The silky fabric, smooth wood sides and artificial floral smells all added up to a terrifying possibility.

I wasn't in Alyce's bedroom.

I was in her coffin.

About the Author

Linda Joy Singleton lives in northern California. She has two grown children and a wonderfully supportive husband who loves to travel with her in search of unusual stories.

She is the author of more than thirty books, including *Dead Girl Walking* (the first in the Dead Girl series), the Strange Encounters series, and The Seer series (all from Llewellyn/Flux). She is also the author of the Regeneration, My Sister the Ghost, and Cheer Squad series. Visit her online at www.LindaJoySingleton.com.

And don't miss the other books in the Dead Girl series,
Dead Girl Walking and *Dead Girl in Love*